NAT DAMON is a write
Los Angeles, CA. He publ

Teach: Time to Reach – Expert Teachers Give Voice to the ~~~~~~
Relational Teaching (Relational Schools Foundation, Cambridge, UK, 2018) and he is the Founding Director of Reach Academics LLC, which serves to strengthen the relationships between all members of K-12 school communities.

Nat grew up in a family of six outside of Boston, MA. He was an English teacher and school administrator for two decades. All the while, he wrote books and screenplays. Nat received a Master's in English Literature from Middlebury College's Bread Loaf School of English and taught in schools in both Massachusetts and California.

While not writing or consulting, Nat often finds himself sailing in Nantucket Sound, traveling to remote areas of the world, or actively involved in organizations aimed at giving voice to the marginalized. This is Nat's first published work of fiction.

TRUE COLORS IN MY ORDINARY WORLD

Nat Damon

SilverWood

Published in 2020 by SilverWood Books

SilverWood Books Ltd
14 Small Street, Bristol, BS1 1DE, United Kingdom
www.silverwoodbooks.co.uk

Copyright © Nat Damon 2020

The right of Nat Damon to be identified as the author of this work has
been asserted in accordance with the Copyright, Designs and
Patents Act 1988 Sections 77 and 78.

All rights reserved. No part of this publication may be reproduced,
stored in a retrieval system, or transmitted in any form or by any means,
electronic, mechanical, photocopying, recording or otherwise,
without prior permission of the copyright holder.

This is a work of fiction. Names, characters, places and incidents either are
products of the author's imagination or are used fictitiously.
Any resemblance to actual events or locales or persons,
living or dead, is entirely coincidental.

ISBN 978-1-78132-919-1 (paperback)
ISBN 978-1-78132-920-7 (ebook)

British Library Cataloguing in Publication Data
A CIP catalogue record for this book is
available from the British Library

Page design and typesetting by SilverWood Books

To Lin

If music be the food of love, play on…

William Shakespeare
Twelfth Night, Act I; Scene I, Line I

To reveal someone's beauty is to reveal their value by giving them time, attention, and tenderness. To love is not just to do something for them but to reveal to them their own uniqueness, to tell them that they are special and worthy of attention.

Jean Vanier, *Becoming Human*

Contents

Brass in Pocket

I didn't hear my alarm. The van picks me up at eight every morning and I didn't hear my alarm this morning. My clock says 7:43. I don't even have my clothes on yet. They are still sitting folded on the sofa across from my bed, next to all my stuffed animals and dolls. It's 7:44. I don't even have my clothes on yet. I'm still in my nightgown because I didn't hear my alarm. I'm going to be late for my van. It picks me up at eight and I don't even have my clothes on yet. Well I can't just stand here staring at my clothes on the sofa next to my stuffed animals. I need to brush my teeth and have breakfast and get my lunchbox from the refrigerator and get in my van. It's 7:44. I don't even have my clothes on yet. I haven't even brushed my teeth. My alarm didn't go off this morning and the van will be here really soon. I need to brush my teeth and put on my clothes and have breakfast downstairs.

I smell coffee from the kitchen. Everyone is downstairs having breakfast except me because my alarm didn't go off. I'm still in my nightgown and I'm going to be so late. I need to brush my teeth and put my clothes on and go downstairs and have breakfast and pick up my lunchbox from the refrigerator and wait for the van that will already be here. I see my clothes on the sofa next to my stuffed animals and my dolls. I folded them and put them there just before going to bed last night at ten o'clock. I will put them on after I brush my teeth in the bathroom. Nobody's using it because they're all downstairs eating breakfast. I can smell the coffee. I hear them all eating breakfast and I'm usually there, too. But this morning I didn't hear my alarm.

"Claire? Come downstairs, honey. Your van's going to be here in ten minutes!" I say something back, something like, *Yes, I'll be right there.* Or, *Of course I know the van is almost here!* Or, *What do you think I'm doing? Just standing here staring at my clothes on the sofa and thinking about how nicely folded they were last night just before ten o'clock, which is my bedtime?*

"Here, Claire, I poured your cereal for you. Sit down and eat it. Your van driver will be here in just a moment."

I sit and stare at the Rice Krispies Mom poured into my cereal bowl. With skim milk. They crackle and pop like the commercial says. I need to eat them, but I don't have any orange juice.

"Let me get you some orange juice."

I put my spoon in the bowl and swirl the Rice Krispies around in a circle. I think about how it's 7:59 and I don't want to get a stomach ache because I wolfed down the Rice Krispies. They float on top of the skim milk and some have fallen out of the bowl, dry and tiny and tan.

"Come on, Claire. You have to eat. The van driver's almost here."

It's 8:01 according to the kitchen clock, which is always late because Dad needs to set it all the time because it gets slow. It's got hands on it, and I'm glad I know how to read the hand clock because if I didn't, I wouldn't know if my van was on time or not.

He must be late.

Mike, my van driver, is never late. The last time he was late, I waited for forty-five minutes, and he told me he'd got a flat tire. He was smiling when he told me this, and it made me wonder whether he'd really got a flat tire or whether he'd just overslept. That's okay if Mike oversleeps. We all do sometimes and it's okay. Mike was tired that day. But he still smiled when he told me the van was late because he got a flat tire.

"Claire Thompson," Mom says, arms on her hips, and huffing. "Please. Eat your cereal and drink your orange juice."

Is my lunchbox in the fridge?

"Yes. You made it last night, remember?"

Tuna fish sandwich and chips and celery and an apple?

"Yes. Now eat up. Everyone's going to be waiting for you."

Everyone's going to be waiting for me if the van is here, but it's not and it's 8:06. I'm not even hungry now because the van is late, and I can't be late for school. But maybe today he really did get a flat tire. Maybe today he will arrive with a new tire on the van so it can get me to school with my friends.

I look down at my Rice Krispies in my cereal bowl. They need to be eaten. It's a long time until lunch and I need to eat my breakfast before the van gets here. I guess I'm lucky that he's late today, too, because I need to eat my breakfast so I won't be hungry at school. When that happens, I don't feel right all day.

"Claire, was there any change to the school schedule today? Was there a note in your lunchbox I was supposed to read?"

I munch on my Rice Krispies and shake my head, no. There was no note. The last note I got from school was last week on Thursday. There's a Valentine's Day Dance on Friday the sixteenth from five to seven and they hope we'll all be there if our parents can sign the permission form on the paper. I remember this because Mom signed it and I returned it the next day like they asked me to. I think everyone's going. It's all everybody is talking about.

I sit on the radiator in front of the dining room window. Mom is on the phone trying to figure out where the van is. It is after 8:25, according to my watch. Not quite 8:30, but it will be soon. I hear Mom talking to someone about the van driver. She sounds urgent. I know she needs to get to work, too.

Besides Mom, there is no other sound in the house. I don't even hear Sandy. He must be outside going to the bathroom or napping in the den on his doggie bed. Every once in a while, I hear a ping sound from the radiator, like someone is hitting it with a stick. That's how quiet it is.

I stare outside at the street, looking up the hill for the van to appear. Mike always comes from up the hill. There are children walking to school. They walk in groups of colorful winter jackets. They all have backpacks or wheelie bags, and they never walk in order. Some seem like they are playing games with each other as they walk down the street. They are all walking to school together and they are talking loud enough that I can hear them through the window and all the way across the street. We have a big front porch and a big front yard and Mike always says that he likes our big driveway because it makes it easy for him to pull the van into the driveway to pick me up at the house. I wonder if the kids are late for school, too. It's probably 8:30 by now, and I think that's late for school for them. They don't act late. They seem like they have all the time in the world, and they seem like they're having fun, so maybe they're not thinking about being late.

It is cold and gray outside. Maybe it will snow. The dining room is very cold. Mom says to me and my brothers to put on a sweater if it's cold. She says she sets the thermostat at sixty-four degrees or else it is too expensive to heat the whole house. The radiator feels warm on my bottom while I wait for the van. Mike's van is always warm. It will feel nice to be warm all over, not just on my bottom where I sit.

Mom, what did the van company say?

The door from the pantry swings open, reminding me that when we were young Kenny hit Danny with the door by accident, he said. But Danny felt it was on purpose and they were angry with each other for a week and the cut on Danny's forehead took a lot longer to heal.

"It's on its way."

That answer means no one knows when he will get here and that I will be late for school along with everyone else in the van. I listen for the van and I stare up the road. I don't like the new color of the house up the street. It's some kind of red but it looks very bright and it stands out. I wonder if they wanted it that way. They probably did. They probably wanted their house to stand out because it will be the only red house on the street. I don't like the color but I'm sure I'll get used to it. The ping-pong table from summer is still on our front porch. Robbie and the twins used to play every day when they got back from day camp. It was like watching dancing when they played together. They are very good ping-pong players, even if Robbie didn't seem like he enjoyed it as much as the twins do. His face never seemed happy playing ping-pong, even though he was as good as his younger twin brothers.

I look down at my watch: 8:40, close to 8:45. I look up through the window. The van has arrived.

*

Where's Jeannie? There are four people in the van and Mike. Dwight, Keith, Cathy and Christine. And Mike our driver. There are usually six people in the van because we have Jeannie. But there is no Jeannie in the van today. She usually sits on the left side in the back next to the window because she likes watching the world go by.

Is she sick?

"She's coming to school with her brother. Her brother is driving her to school," says Cathy. Cathy wears glasses and her haircut looks like that beautiful figure skater named Dorothy's. Cathy doesn't skate, but she lives on a pond where my brothers and my Dad go skating when it is cold outside. I think they could go skating today because it is so cold outside. But it is warm in the van because Mike likes the heat higher than sixty-four degrees. I took off my jacket before sitting down. Mike looks at me through the mirror while he drives.

"We were late because the van wouldn't start. It is so cold out that the van wouldn't start. So I needed to jump it with cables and give it time to warm up. Sorry about that, Claire." He didn't need to apologize. Things happen. But he apologized to me and it felt nice for him to do that. He apologized because I had to wait so long for him to get here. But it's not his fault. He can't help it when the van doesn't work. He takes care of the van as best as he can and he's a very good driver. We have never been in an accident. He makes sure we all have our seatbelts on. He's nice to apologize.

That's okay.

He turns on the radio and the end of the Madonna song plays. Christine and the gang start singing loudly. Cathy shrieks.

16

She loves Madonna. But it was the very end of the song and I know this because of the robots singing about a material world. It ended too quickly. We couldn't even sing the words because the song was ending. We could all sing the words together all of us from the beginning if the song began with us in the van. It's all right, though. We feel better when the music is on even if it's the end of the song and we can't sing to it.

Mike weaves the van with all five of us in it. We are all heading to school. Cathy with her glasses and Dorothy haircut and Madonna. Christine with her rosy cheeks and her buttons. Dwight with his Patriots winter jacket and hat. Keith with his black jacket and briefcase. And me with my pink backpack with my name on it in capital letters, C-L-A-I-R-E.

As we roll and tumble along toward school, with the Boston drivers who Mike thinks should not be allowed on the road, I catch myself in his rear-view mirror. I can't tell if he's looking back at me because of his dark sunglasses. But if he was, he would see me, age 12, my simply brown hair swooped back in tight clips and out of my eyes. He might notice my skin looks clean today because of the new face lotion my Mom is making me try out. He might see the yellowed front tooth behind my smile, the one Dr Brady thinks should be taken out but I really don't think so. I'm not sure what he sees because of his sunglasses hiding his eyes. Perhaps he doesn't see me at all. That wouldn't be unusual from a stranger but it would be from him.

We start singing along with the next song. This is a song Vicki and I listen to and we love it. What is it doing on the radio? I'm excited to hear it. It is one of my favorite songs because the woman's voice is so raspy and she sounds like she's got confidence. We all mumble the words until it gets louder when the chorus comes on. "I'm special, so special. I gotta have some of your attention…*give it to me!*" At that point, we are screaming and laughing and even Mike is smiling so I can see the gold tooth in the back of his smile.

Dance Hall Days

Mom and Dad are going out to dinner with friends tonight, so Mrs. Oops is coming over to babysit. Mrs. Oops has been our babysitter for years. I remember that she has a daughter named Marcia who is in college now. Mrs. Oops loves TV and cooking. She has a wonderful laugh and she's always forgetting where her glasses are. That's how we came up with the name Mrs. Oops. It's really Mrs. Oops, I Forgot My Glasses! One time, she was looking for her glasses when they were on top of her head. I don't know whether she made it up that time in order to get us to laugh. She laughs a lot, and when she does, her cheeks get rosy and her eyes tear up and sparkle. Mrs. Oops isn't young. She is old enough to forget her glasses. But she's very nice and always interested in how I'm doing. She loves Lawrence Welk and Dinah Shore, and sometimes she will watch *The Muppets* with us when we've cleaned our dinner plates.

There was only one time I saw Mrs. Oops get angry and it was when the twins wouldn't go to bed when she needed them to. They were roughhousing, and they deliberately disobeyed her. I think she felt overwhelmed because it wasn't one kid but two. Sometimes the twins can be a handful because there are two of them. Before Mrs. Oops came the next time, Mom and Dad sat down with us and told us to be polite and listen to Mrs. Oops when she wants us to do things. Dad was uncharacteristically firm during this family meeting. He usually goes with the flow. But he said that being polite to Mrs. Oops was very important to him. So that evening Kenny and Danny went to bed without her even needing to ask them to. Robbie and I stayed up and watched *Silver Spoons* with her, giggling when she shook her head at how spoiled it is for a family to have a real train running through their living room.

We never ever ever hid her glasses from her. We knew that would have been too mean and we never wanted to be mean to her.

Mom and Dad like all kinds of music. They play John Denver, Peter, Paul and Mary, and Anne Murray. But they also like different music like disco. And Mom likes classical music, which she plays in the kitchen when she's making dinner. She went through a *Chariots of Fire* phase, and after seeing *Cats*, she played that album constantly until the twins used it as a Frisbee and it was never played again. Dad never yelled at them for that. I think he might have been as tired of *Cats* as we were.

When they come into the kitchen, where we are all eating spaghetti and drinking milk, they look like a million bucks. I love that expression. What is a buck? It's a dollar, I know, but why is it a buck except maybe because the word buck is a funny word. They don't look funny, though. Dad looks so handsome in his suit and tie and Mom is beautiful in her purple dress. They glow together as they walk around us at the dinner table, and they smell fancy. We share a bathroom, so I know that Dad likes Old Spice and Mom likes Chanel No 5. Even though they're from different bottles, they smell good together. Just like Mom and Dad. They smell good together. Especially tonight.

They tell us that Mrs. Oops is sick and they can't get a different babysitter so Robbie will be in charge. He has the number of the place they're going to, and the emergency numbers are by the pantry phone, as they always are. Robbie crosses his arms when Mom and Dad talk to us, looking smug and feeling proud. Kenny and Danny are excited at the idea of their older brother being in charge, sensing as I do that things might get exciting once our parents leave.

The energy crackles as soon as the back door is shut. As the headlights reflect on the garage in smaller beams, Robbie gets up from the table.

"Okay. Who wants a dance-off?"

I have no idea what a dance-off is. I know I love dances, but a dance-off is something I've never heard of. Both the twins shout, "Yes!", and bounce up and down in their chairs. They have no idea what a dance-off is, either. I can tell.

Robbie tells us to clean our plates while he closes the den door. I clear and the twins clean and stack them in record time. What is a dance-off? I will soon find out. But what is it? Kenny knocks on the den door and Robbie tells us to wait a half an hour and that in the meantime we should change into our dance clothes.

"What are dance clothes?" Kenny asks.

Robbie pokes his head out of the door, hiding whatever he was doing inside the den. "Alligator shirt with the collar up. White pants and a colorful belt. And docksiders. And sunglasses. Vuarnets, and if you don't have those, any will do. I know this was a spontaneous plan, so dress code is casual. But the collar has to be up." He shuts the door and the twins run upstairs.

21

*

Robbie told me to wear comfortable clothes, so I'm wearing stretch-waist pants and a colorful T-shirt, which I tuck into my pants. I'm fastening the Velcro on my sneakers when I find him at my doorway, out of breath.

"Okay. I think I got everything set up downstairs. You look nice."

He takes my hairbrush off the dresser and starts brushing my hair. At this time, it's dark brown and shoulder length. I'm excited to dance. I'll have fun with my brothers. Robbie is clearly excited about this.

"Perfect. You look great! Do you want make-up?"

I shake my head. *No, I'm fine.* He gives a thumbs up and says, "The club opens in five minutes!"

I look at myself in the mirror. I always look better when Robbie brushes my hair. It looks shiny and wavy. I can't make it do that on my own.

I get downstairs and the dance-off is a bust. Kenny, Danny and Robbie are in the corner by the record player looking upset with each other. Kenny says hi and says that I look pretty. I see that Robbie has put a lot of effort into making the den look fun. There are glow sticks and I don't know where he found the disco ball, but there it is, pinned into the beam in the ceiling, reflecting white lights all around. Robbie has a bandana around his head and sunglasses and his collar is up. He looks good – like he belongs on the poster of that band in his bedroom. The one that has five men wearing bandanas and colorful clothes. I think one of them is wearing make-up.

"We're having a problem with the music," Kenny tells me.

22

I take a handful of Doritos from the bowl on the coffee table.

"I just don't think this music works for the club. Let's try this one." Robbie holds up a record that has a picture of two men and two women. They're all attractive, and the background is blue and white and simple.

"No!" Danny says. "I want John Denver."

Robbie looks at Kenny and rolls his eyes. Kenny grabs some Doritos from my bowl. I think of offering them to the other two but they're in the middle of their argument.

"John Denver isn't dance music! I want to play dance music! That's the whole point of a dance *club*?" I'm confused because Robbie sounded like he was asking a question, but really he wasn't. The silence that follows isn't very enjoyable. Danny sits on the sofa in a huff and Kenny keeps eating from the bowl of Doritos. I don't think Robbie is thinking about food at all. He is messing around with the record player and turning his back on all of us.

Just then, the sound of someone sweeping a piano is followed by heavenly voices and a disco rhythm that makes anyone with a beating heart want to get up and dance. Before I know it, Kenny, Danny and Robbie are dancing to the music, singing, "You can dance, you can jive, having the *time of your life*…" Robbie is leading the entourage, moving like I've never seen him before. He is without bones, hands reaching out to me to come dance with him. The twins are in their own worlds, just happy to be there with smiles on their faces. Suddenly, the disco ball, the glow sticks and the streamers all come together through the music and the joy. The den has become a place for my brothers to be free from our parents, school, friends, sports and everything that makes them feel upset. Even Sandy joins in, standing in the middle of the room, panting and watching us all go crazy.

23

Forever Young

My twin brothers are five years younger than me. Mom and Dad always say what a gift it was to have two at once when they thought it would just be one. When they were very young, the twins had something wrong with their heads and they were in the hospital. Robbie and I stayed with Granny and I don't know where Mom and Dad were. I think at the hospital. I don't remember much about that time except Granny getting stung by a bumblebee on her belly button when she was gardening. She didn't cry.

Kenny and Danny are always playing around. Kenny wears red and Danny wears blue. This is so that everyone can tell them apart. I don't know if Kenny chose red and Danny chose blue. It might not have been their choice. I think it was Mom and Dad's choice. All their lives, Kenny is the red one and Danny is the blue one. Robbie says his favorite color is green, but I think it's actually blue. His favorite things are the ocean and he loves to lie on the ground and look at the sky. I wonder if he knows this. Maybe he didn't say anything when Mom and Dad told him that Danny is the blue twin. But the twins don't seem to mind being red and blue, maybe because it means less people calling them the Thompson Twins and laughing.

In every family picture we have on the walls of the stairway Kenny is red and Danny is blue. Robbie wears green. I wear whatever color I want because I'm a girl and everyone knows me as Claire.

I saw a special on TV about animals and they showed otters playing in the water. There were two of them. They roughhoused and rolled around on the mudflats and they were identical to each other. If they had mouths that smiled, they would be smiling. I could hear them making sounds like laughing, and I started laughing to myself watching the otters play. They reminded me of my twin brothers.

Kenny and Danny are always tumbling around. There they are in the basement wrestling each other. There they are in the front hallway beating each other up with Nerf bats. There they are in Granny's pool, trying to push each other's head under the water. They are always messing around.

Danny is always smiling. His teacher calls him carefree. I can see that. His eyes are wide open and he asks a lot of questions and his eyebrows are raised. His face is wide like his open eyes. Kenny is quiet and thoughtful. His eyes make you know he is listening carefully. They are narrow and focused. Kenny doesn't need attention. His teacher says he is a deep thinker with a warm heart. I can see that, too. It's fun to see the twins together because even though they are different they act like they're the same. But that's only when they are together. Really they are very different.

In the cold weather, Dad hoses down the driveway and turns it into a hockey rink. It will be like this for as long as the ice is not melted. Kenny, Danny, and sometimes friends of theirs will skate around with their hockey sticks and play hockey in the driveway. They break windows on the garage and one time they broke the kitchen window and Mom yelled at them because she was washing dishes only moments beforehand. They asked Robbie for a loan to pay for it from his paper route money. He said no way and that if they wanted they could do his paper route for him for a month. They said they would but Dad said they were too young. So I don't know how they paid for the broken window.

They never roughhouse on the ice. They hit each other and try to make each other fall, but they don't wrestle. I guess that's because they know better than that. Or maybe they are just careful after Mom broke four ribs by slipping on the driveway. She slipped and fell because the driveway was a hockey rink and she was in a hurry. I don't think Mom likes the hockey rink. She probably wishes it were always a driveway.

"Don't touch the sugar!" *But I always put sugar on my Special K.* Kenny slides the sugar container away. Danny gives me the 'shh' sign with his finger on his lips. How am I going to eat my Special K without sugar? It's not Rice Krispies. I only like Special K with sugar. Maybe we're out of sugar? I reach for the bowl and almost remove the lid to see, but this time Danny takes it from me. He didn't need to say anything, but still... I don't know what they are up to and I feel upset that I don't have sugar at breakfast.

Robbie comes downstairs and pours some Raisin Bran for himself. As he's about to take his first bite, Danny asks, "Don't you want some sugar?"

Robbie says, "It's Raisin Bran."

Danny repeats himself. "But don't you want some sugar?"

"No, I don't want some sugar. Why do you care so much if

26

I have sugar on my cereal?" He reaches for the sugar bowl. "Give me that."

Danny keeps it to himself. "No."

"What's going on? Kenny? Come on. Why aren't you giving me the sugar?"

The twins look at each other. "Fine. We filled it with salt. April Fool."

Robbie rolls his eyes. "Oh, come on. You can't do better than that?" He sees the twins have sad expressions. "Hey. It was a good try. Just next time take away the Raisin Bran. That stuff is loaded with sugar."

"We can still see if Dad puts salt in his coffee."

"I don't think that would be a good idea. Come on. Let's change it back."

Suddenly, Robbie bolts up from the table. "How can it be eight already?" He is about to grab his backpack when he freezes and stares at the twins. "April Fool, right?" He smirks. They nod, beaming in satisfaction.

I look at the clock and it says 8:00. I need to fix that and make it right. I need clocks to tell the right time, even if it's April Fool's Day. I get up and try to take the clock off the wall.

"Leave it up!" Danny says.

"No, let's reset it. Joke's over." Robbie helps wind the hands to show the right time. I feel more relaxed once the clock is up on the wall telling the right time. I look at my watch to make sure it's the same time as the clock and the microwave clock and the clock on the stove. All the clocks say 7:50. Except the clock on the microwave. The clock on the microwave says 8:00 still. I don't know how to set the clock on the microwave. I feel jumpy so I go upstairs and get my bag ready for school.

*

When I get home from school, I'm greeted by Mrs. Oops. *Where are my brothers?*

"They're still at school. So are your parents."

Why would they still be at school? I look at the clock on the kitchen wall. It says 4:14. *Why are they at school?*

"They pulled a stunt, honey. They tried switching classrooms and the teachers caught them. Because of April Fool's."

Oh, I see. I start unpacking my backpack. I take out my lunchbox and open it. The containers need to be washed so I start rinsing them in the kitchen sink. I smell the leftover tuna fish from my sandwich and I see the tiny little orange crumbs from my Doritos. I throw away the stem from my green grapes and I open the thermos and empty the rest of the milk.

"You are so responsible, you know that? I don't even have to be here."

I nod my head because I'm busy cleaning my lunchbox at the sink. Mrs. Oops is looking at the back of my head because I can feel it. I can also see her reflected in the window the twins broke when they were playing ice hockey. Once finished with my cleaning, I make my way to the stairs.

"Would you like some tea?" Mrs. Oops asks.

I keep walking. I need to go upstairs to my room. I need to go to the bathroom. I need to change out of my dirty, wet socks because my boots aren't waterproof. I need to get things done.

No, thanks.

As I walk up the stairs, I think about the twins and what must have happened at school today. I know they got in trouble. But I feel giggly about it inside anyways.

Cruel Summer

My skin feels chilly and I hold my breath tight. The water is thick and heavy and it makes my arms feel achy. It stings my eyes and everything looks blurry and bright. My arms ache and my legs keep kicking. *Keep kicking, Claire. Keep kicking.* Okay, I keep kicking. And my arms push and pull me toward the other side. My breath is running out even though I took in a lot of it. I turn my head to the side and inhale quickly. The sun in the sky blinds my squinty eyes at that moment, and I close them tight. I see spots. My arms push me and my fingertips touch the other side. Made it. I stop kicking. My legs feel achy and good. My arms feel the same. Inside, I feel happy and I smile.

"Great job, Claire! Wow – you made it all the way to the other side of the pool!"

It's Sally. I know it's Sally even if I can't see her clearly because of the water in my eyes and the sun blinding my vision. It's Sally because of her robin-like voice and because she's always supportive. She makes me feel like I can do things. She makes me feel like I can do anything. Sally wears big, round glasses that turn into sunglasses when she's at the pool. She tells me she doesn't know how it happens. It's magic, she thinks. Sally believes it is magic. I think she's right. I made it to the other side of the pool. My arms ache and I can't see clearly. But Sally's shadow cools me and I know I have made it to the other side of the pool. It is my first time doing this. It's my first time swimming to the other side of the pool and Sally is proud of me.

I have a lot of pools to swim in. There are two here at Morningside Day Camp. I'm in the blue pool. There is also the gray pool, which I don't like. The gray pool is rough and my hands and feet get scars from it sometimes. Granny's pool is like the blue pool. It is blue and light and smooth to touch. There is also the Newberrys' pool on the Cape and I always thought it was great that they had a pool and a beach and an ocean to swim in. I prefer the pool. But having other options is nice. My friend Dwight has a pool and his pool is always fun because there is a diving board and Dwight uses it all the time to make a splash. His pool is a funny shape. It's not like other pools with corners. It's not a circle, either. It's a funny shape. It's hard to describe. But it's still a fun pool to swim in. During the winter, I swim in the Parkland Rec indoor pool. It's kind of like swimming in all the other pools but it has a roof on it because in the winter it is too cold outside. That pool also makes steam and it smells very strong like chemicals or something that isn't cleared away by the air and the breeze.

I'm swimming in the blue pool because Dad works here. He works here in the summer. He works with the counselors and talks to parents and plays with the kids. At the end of the day, everyone sits on the grass and listens to him before they get into their carpools. Sometimes in the winter Dad speaks to parents in front of a slideshow from the summer before. My favorite part of sitting on the grass at the end of the day is when Susan the music counselor sings a song with us on her guitar. Susan has a beautiful voice – almost as beautiful as Vicki's, but no one has a singing voice as beautiful as Vicki does. My least favorite part of sitting on the grass at the end of the day is sitting on the grass. It makes my skin itch and I scratch it for hours and end up getting scabs.

On this day, Sally gave me an orange popsicle for swimming across the blue pool. She told me that I would swim to the end and back by the end of the summer. While we were all sitting on the grass at the end of the day, Sally stood up and made an announcement about me swimming to the other end of the pool. Everybody clapped. I saw Dad clapping very hard standing off to the side. It was a nice feeling. Afterwards, my counselors for the Guppy group reminded us that there would be a cookout after camp tomorrow. I knew about it already, but sometimes people can forget because they are busy thinking about other things.

"It's going to be a game of Marco Polo!" The group of Guppies gets excited while sitting on the hot stairs in front of the gray pool. Marco Polo is a game when someone closes her eyes and everyone else has their eyes open. The one with her eyes closed says, "Marco!" and the others say, "Polo!" The girl with her eyes closed tries to tag one of the girls who can see. Everyone has fun playing even if they are the girl with her eyes closed. It's fun to play tag in the pool. I like jumping around, and sometimes I get very excited and need to remind myself to calm down. I do that pretty easily most times.

"We will be in the gray pool." I look over at the blue pool and see two men in the same uniform squatting next to the water with plastic tools in their hands. They must be testing the chlorine. I've seen this before, but usually it's on weekends when Dad brings us to camp in order to test things. Like chlorine.

It's fine, though. I'll just stay on the shallow side of the pool and be careful that my feet don't scrape on the bottom.

While playing Marco Polo, the energy in the pool feels like we've all turned into electric eels. I see sparks in the water and feel tiny shocks from the churning water. Every once in a while, I swallow water in the wrong way and I cough it out. The volume at the pool is nearly deafening because everyone is screaming, including me. The water in the pool really looks like it's filled with electric eels, splashing and feeding on each other. It's not the same as a group of otters.

All of this is making me feel like a break. I walk up the steps in the shallow end of the gray pool, gripping the hot metal railing for balance. The dizziness from being in the water always makes me feel wobbly. I walk along the side of the pool toward my pink and green watermelon towel to dry off. I need to dry off because I spent a long time in the pool and I'm soaking wet and the sun is beginning to set because it's behind the trees. I see my towel and will use it to dry off. The pool looks like it is boiling water from the bubbles and splashes and noises from the other girls. I'm glad to be out and away from Marco Polo because it feels too much.

The thud on the middle of my back isn't as painful as the giggles that come with it. The water feels cold and angry as I sink to the bottom of the deep end. I hold my breath, as much breath as I have inside, because I wasn't told to take a deep breath. The push just came from out of nowhere. It came from the giggles. It is dark and cold at the bottom of the pool. It is also silent. It sounds nice on my ears and in my head. I need to get a new breath and I need to get to the top again. But I'm dizzy and I don't see anything in the water except shadows and light. The silence feels nice, though.

The sound of another thud above me is followed by the tickling of bubbles all over my face. Hands firmly grip my shoulders and move down my side. The water thrusts alongside me. The bubbles tickle. The water thrusts. I'm secure and safe in these strong hands. I see the light. I feel the surface break. I'm held, now breathing, now back on the surface expecting to be surrounded by noise and din.

But it's as silent on the top of the water as on the bottom. The girls are frozen with wet hair slicked back. They look like statues looking at me. Their eyes all look the same. They are scared and they are sad. They want to explain what happened but they can't. It just happened. I survey the faces staring at me like statues. I want to tell them it's okay. But that doesn't feel right, so I don't.

The silence is interrupted by muffled sniffles coming from the stairs. Three girls are crying. Two counselors are bent over them, pointing and using their arms in jerky motions. One points at me over and over while talking at the girls. The sobbing can be heard all over the pool area. It feels uncomfortable. I feel like I caused them to cry. I don't know why I have this feeling. Maybe I got too excited in the water. Or I didn't play the game just right. Or I shouldn't have gotten out of the water to dry off in the middle of the game. It could be any of these, but if it is, I only feel a little bit better.

You Can't Always Get What You Want

Mom slipped and broke four ribs because the driveway turned into an ice skating rink. She was hurrying to a meeting at church and she slipped. It doesn't hurt she says. Only when she laughs. So we try not to make her laugh because we don't want her to hurt. But she laughs sometimes anyway, and when she does, she presses her hands to her ribs. The harder she laughs, the more it hurts. I see her eyes well with tears and they are tears from laughing, but we must make sure they are not also tears from hurt. Mom spends a lot of time resting because there isn't anything to do when you break four ribs. There is no bandage that makes them get better quickly. You just have to wait it out, Dad told Danny at the breakfast table.

Dad is in the kitchen a lot more now that Mom is resting. We are eating a lot of pea soup, and the milk carton is always left open on the table. I'm always putting milk back in the refrigerator where it belongs or it gets sour. I don't know how Dad and my brothers don't see the milk on the table. They don't see the clocks aren't telling the same time or the coats that slipped off the hooks in the mud room, either. And the cap on the salad dressing needs to be closed, with the leftover lettuce in a bag to go back to the vegetable drawer in the refrigerator. And the cereal box that one of my brothers opened wrong now it spills Cheerios all over the table when I try to pour it into my bowl. I'm busier in the kitchen because Mom broke her ribs and she's upstairs a lot resting. Otherwise she would notice these things and help me keep the kitchen the way it should be. But nobody's perfect and I can do these things.

Mom slipped and broke four ribs the day after Christmas. Robbie said at least it didn't happen before Christmas or Santa would've had a hard time delivering his presents. The twins didn't understand what Mom's ribs had to do with Santa. I didn't either but I know that Robbie reads a lot of books and talks with big words so he must be saying something that is correct. After Robbie said that about Santa having difficulty and the twins asking what difference it would make, and Dad jumping in and saying, "I don't think that makes any difference" and Robbie suddenly going silent, after all of that happening at the same time, I realized that maybe Robbie was wrong and more. I could see the dark under his eyes when he looked at the ground after Dad said that it doesn't make any difference and all that matters is that what Robbie said about Mom's ribs and Santa didn't go over well.

After she slipped and broke four ribs the day after Christmas, Mom spent a lot of time getting better. While she was doing this, the rest of us were keeping a tight ship. That is the way Dad told us to be. What mattered is that we keep a tight ship because with the captain out of commission it's up to us to keep things clean and orderly, he said. This is what he would do in the Navy. Keep things moving along shipshape. Besides the little things like the milk carton, we were doing our best and we were making him proud. When Dad is proud of us, he sits with us and tells us stories about his years in the Navy. When Dad is proud of us, he tells us stories while smoking his pipe. The sweet smell of tobacco mixes with his Old Spice, and he is our father.

At the end of telling us about when he was docked in Singapore, Dad told us we are going to Treasure Cay. Treasure Cay is in the Bahamas. Robbie and I went to the Bahamas when we were young and the twins were getting better and Granny got stung by the bumblebee. We went with our next-door neighbors on the Cape, the Sumners. It was a fun trip. We spent a lot of time on the balcony of a nice house that looked out on a lot of boats. Robbie loved the hammock and he would read The Hardy Boys and I would paint shells in watercolors. Once Robbie climbed a coconut tree with the biggest smile I've ever seen. After he climbed the tree, we found a coconut on the sand. Mr. Sumner took out a knife and broke the coconut open at the top. We drank from the coconut and it was sour. Mr. Sumner then fed us pieces he carved from the coconut. I remember coconuts from Treasure Cay. I wonder whether the twins will think coconuts taste good when we are at Treasure Cay in April.

"Okay, this is what we will do," Robbie says at our very important meeting in the beach house living room. We are together because Robbie says it is important for us to thank our parents for such a great week together in Treasure Cay. He is right that it was a great week. We swam every day, we sailed and motorboated, we found starfish and coconuts, I painted shells and we all got rest and relaxation. All of us got a tan and had a fun time. Mom felt better because she played a lot of tennis and she had good walks on the beach with Aunt Penny. We took this trip with Dad's family. It was Gammy and Grandpops, Uncle Jude and Aunt

36

Penny, our cousins Bryce and Maisie, Uncle Phil, and us. That's a lot of family together so we also had a babysitter from up the street with us whose name is Katie.

Robbie wants us all to sing for them to thank them. The twins don't like that idea. They say they can't sing and after Robbie says that everyone can sing, they get louder about not being able to sing. Danny says it's a bad idea and Kenny says there's no way he is going to sing. Bryce and Maisie are quiet, probably because they're cousins and not brother and sister. Bryce is close to Robbie's age and Maisie is around the twins' age. We had fun with them this week. They agree with the twins because they'd say anything to support Robbie's idea.

We try to come up with another way to thank them. While we do this, Robbie becomes quiet and sits down while the twins take over. They don't want to sing. Bryce and Maisie stay quiet and the twins keep arguing. Then Katie our babysitter says, "I think I might have the answer." She leaves the room and returns moments later with an eight-track tape. "There's nothing some British blues with a gospel choir can't fix."

The song starts with a choir that is just kids. It is like angels. So clear. So pure. The harmony in the background is lovely. Then the singing stops and a guitar sound takes over. Strings being strummed and it sounds clean. Then a man's voice. It sounds intense. Sad and hopeful and honest. Then the chorus begins and I understand how it fits with the sound of the man. The chorus is a message and it is true. And the piano joins in. Then all of a sudden, the song opens up and there is drumming and some background singers who are not kids. They have voices that blend like warm caramel. I find myself lost in this song from beginning to end. Everyone in the room is silent all the way until the choir builds and soars so high I'm sure the voices are touching heaven. The chorus invites us all in, like it opens up into a tunnel that gets wider and welcomes us in and guides us higher and higher with it. I want to cry and I want to sing and I want to see the rainbow that is stenciled in my ears.

After the song ends, Robbie jumps off the sofa. "This is *it!*" He then instructs everyone about what they will do. Kenny and Danny get tennis racket guitars. Maisie gets the coffee table piano. Bryce gets the upside-down wastebasket as drums. Robbie holds the red plastic baseball fat-bat upside-down as a microphone.

"What about Claire?" Katie asks. *Yes, what about me?*

"Claire? You and Claire are backup singers, obviously." Katie looks at me, smiles, and says, "Awright, girlfriend. Let's work on some moves."

The next evening, Katie pushes the buttons on the eight-track machine and opens the curtains. I see the grown-ups all sitting down with their cocktails and cigarettes and watching us with clear eyes and suntans. Kenny and Danny mimic the choir as the music spreads out above the adults and into the starry night. Robbie struts to the front of the stage with his fat-bat microphone and becomes someone I've never seen before. The way he moves is like he is becoming the rhythm and I feel like I want to join him. I don't because I know that I have a job to do. But even standing behind him I can sense that Robbie has become the man with the sad and hopeful and honest voice. And when the chorus flies out to the moon and beyond, I'm certain Robbie's eyes are teary with the truth of the chorus. I'm special. But I also can't always get what I want. I think Robbie is the same as me. And I think deep inside he knows it, too.

What I Like About You

Sometimes people shine a light from their faces. It doesn't matter if they are a man or a woman. They shine so I can feel their shine. They are like the sun in the Raisin Bran commercial on TV. When you're around them, their face feels warm on your face. It's like the sun but it's more than the sun. The sun feels hot on my skin. The warmth from these certain people feels soothing-warm inside my face and into my heart and through my fingers. They are men or women. They are tall or short. They are special or regular. These people who make me feel warm to my fingers are not very many. There is one person who made me feel warm to my fingers the first time I met her. My friend Vicki wears jeans that are tight on her legs and T-shirts that are tight on her tummy. Her light isn't trapped in the tightness of her jeans and her T-shirt. It doesn't matter what clothes she's wearing. She is able to let her light shine and let it shine, let it shine, let it shine.

Vicki is my friend from Wellesley College. She goes to Wellesley College. I am too young for college because I go to St Coletta's. I have another nine years at St Coletta's and then I will be 21 and I will go to work somewhere. I won't go to college because my parents told me I will go to work. That's all right because Vicki tells me college is hard with classes and reading and she likes our friendship because it gets her mind off of her work. Whenever I need a babysitter, Vicki is there. Yet she is more than a babysitter because she shines around me. And that's how I know she is more of a friend.

"Turn it up, Claire! I'm gonna let it shine, let it shine, let it shine! Sing with me!" I do as she says. I turn up the knob on the radio and I start to sing. *This little light of mine...* Vicki speeds up her car named Doris and we weave around the bends of the road and the tree branches are throwing shade in flickers. She leans forward and rolls down her window and props her elbow in the window frame and lets the wind rush through her curly hair combed by her fingertips. She sings louder. "I'm gonna let it shiiiiiiiiiiine!" I can't hear my own voice with the wind in the window and the volume turned up and her voice loud and rich with excitement. Feelings are stirring deep inside me like butterfly wings but not in my tummy. I roll down my window, too.

The police car makes us pull over and stop. It's a feeling like when Danny scratched the needle on Kenny's *Star Wars* record and everything froze. That was one of the biggest fights I'd ever seen. I don't like to think about it. When the police car makes us pull over and stop, Vicki says, "Well, doesn't this just put a crank in our day!" I have no idea what it means to put a crank in our day. It must have something to do with a bump in the road.

"Oh, Officer. I'm so sorry! This little lady over here, she's an American version of Sarah Brightman! It's really all her fault." The whole time Vicki is talking it is like she's singing. The whole time Vicki is talking, the officer's eyes crinkle at the corners. The whole time Vicki is talking, there isn't going to be a fight. The whole time Vicki is talking, I see her hand pat the officer's hand gripping her window frame. The whole time Vicki is talking, I know that things are not going to end up bad.

While the officer does his thing in his car behind us, Vicki reaches into the space in between our seats. She takes out her pack of Virginia Slims and says, "Do you mind if Doris and I take a smoke break?" *No, I don't mind.* She looks at me like she knows it's not healthy to smoke but she deserves it and Doris has taken us very far today and being pulled over by the nice policeman was a crank in our day. The windows are down and I don't mind that she smokes. I mind it a lot when other people smoke. Except Dad and his pipe, which smells just right with his Old Spice.

The radio plays a tape from *Godspell*, which is a lot like *Joseph and the Amazing Technicolor Dreamcoat* but the songs are more popular. Lake Waban shimmers in front of us as we lie down in our swimsuits with our tummies on our towels and the sun on our backs. There are the occasional ants that irritate my skin, but Vicki doesn't complain about them and I try to learn from her. The castle looms on the hill over us and we are interrupted by the occasional jogger on this humid, white summer day. It's a day that feels like there will be ice cream at the end even though we haven't talked about ice cream. It's one of those days.

Vicki reaches for a Virginia Slims cigarette. While taking a deep inhale, she closes her eyes and holds the smoke in her lungs for what feels like a minute. As she exhales the smoke in one long, blue-gray chimney that lingers in a dissipating fog cloud around us, she turns to me, her eyes hooking into my own.

"Just be you, Claire." She reaches out and pats my back like

Dad patting Sandy. I look at the grass and see two ants on the same long piece of grass. They freeze their movement, as if posing for a picture. I feel Vicki's eyes still gazing at my face. Her other hand is patting me, then resting on the swell of my back. "I'm lucky to have you as my friend." I watch the ants, which are now chewing the blade of grass. One tries to climb over the other, yet the other won't let it. They start bumping into each other on purpose. "Be strong and be fabulous." What is she talking about? Strong like the ants? "Fabulous" describes people who dress in bold colors and are followed by hundreds of people. I'm not strong like the ants. When I get angry, I shake inside and I clench my fists and stare at them until the anger goes away. When I dress, I wear regular-colored clothes. I'm not fabulous or strong. But I hope Vicki and I are friends forever. I like thinking about that and I fold my arms together and rest my head on them, facing away from Vicki's eyes and comforted by the hand on my back.

As I drift into sleep, I hear her sing in my direction in a voice that makes me feel like I'm safe and protected like the hand on my back. I allow the song to penetrate my skin and burrow into my heart as it comes from her heart and makes a bridge between us.

> *The water is wide, I cannot get o'er*
> *Neither have I wings to fly*
> *Give me a boat that can carry two*
> *And both shall cross my true love and I*

"Weren't you at the rally?" An unfamiliar voice jolts me out of my deep sleep. I lift my head and squint at the woman who stands in front of us talking to Vicki. They engage in a conversation for a long time and as I rest my head back on my folded arms, I realize

42

that their conversation is perfect background noise because it is about things I don't know. So I listen to the words, paying attention to the rhythm and their variety. I find myself falling back asleep, hoping to resume my dream about finding a boat the other side of the water.

When I wake up again, there is a group of women sitting around us. Vicki is sitting up cross-legged. The woman who woke me up is sitting next to her and there are two other women in the group talking with their arms and pausing every so often, and I hear the birds chirping. I smell something unfamiliar and off-putting. It's smoky and sour and it comes from a messy, wrinkled cigarette being passed around from woman to woman. When Vicki reaches for the cigarette, I see her underarm hair poking out because she's only wearing her bathing suit still. The other women are wearing T-shirts and none are skinny and that is okay. The only thing that bothers me is the smell of the cigarette and the loud voices they use. It's funny that when someone starts laughing everyone else starts laughing, too. The funny thing is that they don't know what they are laughing about.

One of them turns to me. "Claire, right?" I nod yes. "You're part of the sisterhood, too." Yes, I agree. I'm a sister. Robbie, Kenny and Danny are my brothers, so I'm a sister. *Do you have brothers and sisters, too?* The woman says, "Only sisters, I'm afraid. And that's all right with me!" She laughs and the others start laughing, too. Vicki's face is red and I hope it's because of her laughing and not because she got too much sun. The other woman signals to me. "Come join us! You're part of the sisterhood now, Claire." I look to Vicki, who nods in approval. Yes, it's all right. Yes, I can join the sisterhood. It's time I stopped napping. I want to be awake with Vicki and her friends. They seem nice and they invited me to be their sister, too. I see an opening in the circle, and the woman is patting the grass. She wants me to join her and be a sister with her. She wants me to join their group and on such a nice day outside, I think it sounds like a very good idea.

Just Like Heaven

I step around Donna's wheelchair holding my backpack in my left hand. Getting out of the van is tricky for me because of Donna's wheelchair, but I plan ahead how to get around it and usually it works out just fine. Donna's wheelchair is metal and blue and it sits between my seat and the van door. It's fun to sit next to Donna in her wheelchair because Donna talks with a Boston accent. Donna lived in West Roxbury and she moved to Weston a few months ago. Donna is new to the van, and we have gotten used to it. She is funny with her accent, and there is room in the van for her wheelchair. I step around her and hold my backpack in my left hand and hop out of the van and wave goodbye to Mike. He toots the horn back at me very quickly so it doesn't disturb the Clintons across the street and I walk up the two stairs to the back door of my house. It is still winter so Dad hasn't replaced the storm door with the screen door yet. That usually happens sometime around Easter and it always means that summer is around the corner.

Donna says that summer is her least favorite season. I ask, *Why isn't it winter because of the ice, and it's slippery?* Donna says it's worse to be stuck in her wheelchair with the sun and the heat, and the metal of the wheelchair gets very hot and it burns her arms and sometimes the back of her legs. She says sometimes she sits and waits a long time for her Mom or whoever told her to wait here for a sec while I'm in the store. Today, it's still winter and I'm happy for Donna that she doesn't worry about slipping on the ice in her wheelchair. She's very good at moving it around to get to where she wants to go. I'm very happy nobody tells her to wait here for a sec, because it's winter outside. I hope this summer no one tells her to wait here for a sec and then comes back a long time later.

I shuffle into the mud room and drop my backpack and bend down to un-Velcro my boots and I hear Granny's voice and I feel tingly with excitement. *Hi, Granny!* I'm not even done yet with my boots. I say it again. It's Wednesday. Granny comes by to pick me up every Wednesday to bring me to her house for the night. *Hi, Granny!* My warm sneakers are on and I walk into the kitchen and find her sitting at the breakfast table with the twins and Robbie. *Hi, Granny!*

She is always perfectly dressed. She speaks in a way I can understand. Her smile is from her eyes and her mouth. She asks questions and makes us all feel like we are the most important people in the world. She is Mom's mom, and she treats us like we are her own children. Her black and gray hair is perfectly done. Her glasses are always fixed to the bridge of her nose. She wears a silver pin on her pink sweater and blue pants. She smells like Mom's Chanel No 5 and wool. The only make-up she wears is lipstick. Being around Granny is like being around Queen Elizabeth. There are no surprises and she even speaks in an almost English accent.

"Why hello, Claire! Would you care to join us for some afternoon tea?" Her voice has an accent that's like you take Donna's

46

accent and smooth it out with a rolling pin and cover it with a dishcloth. It is long and it is delightful. Granny passes me a teacup and saucer. There is already tea in the teacup so she must have thought about me before I got home. It is a nice feeling to be thought of before I come home, while I'm away. I reach over for a sugar cube and plop one in. Granny leans over and pours in the milk. I take my little teaspoon and start stirring it in circles.

Robbie says, "No, Claire. Never circles. Stir your tea up and down like I'm doing." I watch Robbie go back and forth with his teaspoon, making a clink every time it hits the side of his teacup. I try to do the same thing but the tea spills over the side. Still, I guess it's better and that must be why there is a saucer. Danny exclaims, "I love drinking my tea like this!" He lifts his teacup to his mouth and his pinkie finger is outstretched. Granny tells him he does not need to lift his pinkie, and that not spilling the tea is good enough. He nods and does it again, this time keeping his pinkie finger wrapped around the handle like the other fingers. Granny nods in approval and Kenny smiles to himself, knowing he's doing it perfectly. Time spent with Granny makes us feel good. She adds light to our lives.

Staying Wednesday night at Granny's house is like watching a play and you're on the stage with the actors but you're still in the audience. Granny is reheating meatloaf and making fresh salad. Grandy is watching the news on television with a gin and tonic in his hand. He makes his own gin and tonics because he says Granny doesn't make them right. He makes his own gin and tonics at the bar, and I only go to the bar when I need something from the refrigerator like a Sprite, which is my favorite soda. Otherwise, only Grandy goes to the bar. He makes Granny her cocktails because he makes them better than anyone else.

When I go to Granny's house on Wednesday night, I usually bring my pad of paper and markers so I can sit down and not trip over the dogs. Hotsie and Echo are corgis. I know this because Granny and Grandy don't call them dogs, they call them corgis. Echo is an orange corgi with white paws. Hotsie is a black and white corgi with a hearing problem. Hotsie is older than Echo, but Hotsie gets jealous when someone pats Echo and not him. When Hotsie gets jealous, he barks over and over again. I think Hotsie's bark is loud because he doesn't hear it well. I try not to pat either corgi because I don't like it when Hotsie barks over and over again. It distracts all of us from what we are doing and it makes Granny and Grandy upset.

Granny's house is small even though it is on a hill with a pond and a barn that is used for games like pool and darts. On the other side of the hill is the pool, which is like the blue pool at Morningside. Inside the house, the ceilings are very low and even I feel like I could bump my head in some doorways. I can touch the ceiling anywhere in the house if I get on my tiptoes. The only problem with the house is the stairs are very steep. I need to walk down them carefully because I get dizzy going down stairs anyway and these stairs are very steep so it doesn't help. I go down stairs on both feet so when my right foot touches the next step my left foot touches the same step before I go to the next step with my right foot. It annoys my brothers to be behind me when I go down the stairs, but it is better than being rushed and falling because I get dizzy doing down stairs. Grandy calls me a cat because I have no problem going up stairs but going down stairs takes forever, he says.

*

48

A long time before I started spending Wednesday nights at Granny's house I was staying at Granny's house with Robbie because the twins were in the hospital with something wrong with their heads. It was the summer and Granny was outside gardening. Granny was weeding the rose garden and I saw a bumblebee land on her yellow alligator shirt that she was gardening in. I didn't see anything happen except it landed on her. But she said "Ouch!" anyway, and I could tell it stung her because she slapped her tummy and the bee fell to the ground next to her gardening shovel. Granny lifted her shirt just enough to see a red dot below her bellybutton. She took her fingers and squeezed the red dot so that it became pink all around it. She pulled something out and flicked it to the dirt. Afterwards, she looked at me and it was the first and only time I ever saw tears in her eyes that were not from laughter. "It's all right, Claire," she said, as if to herself. "These things happen and I'm just glad it didn't happen to you." When she said that it made me feel good and bad. It made me feel good because she must love me very much. It made me feel bad because if she didn't want me to feel it like she did, it must have hurt a lot.

The time when Robbie and I stayed at Granny's house when the twins were in the hospital was a quiet time. Mom and Dad visited but only very quickly because they had to be back at the hospital. One time, Dad took Robbie to the hospital to see the twins and when Robbie got back I asked him about it. He said he didn't want to tell me about it because he didn't want me to feel sad. This made me feel like the bumblebee with Granny. It made me feel good because he must love me very much. It made me feel bad because if he didn't want me to feel it like he did, it must have made Robbie very sad.

One time, I found a picture of the twins when they were in the hospital. Mom, Dad, Robbie and the twins were up in Vermont and I was in the house with Mrs. Oops. I needed to find some tape, so I went to the basement area where Mom wraps presents with tape. I saw an open photo album that was being worked on and there were pictures from when I was very young. Some pictures were very happy like one of me and Robbie hanging upside down on a jungle gym with our uncles holding us. There was a picture of me with Mom and Granny (the Three Clarissas, because our names are all Clarissa even though Mom is called Rissie by her friends and on her mail). There was a picture of Robbie blowing up a beach ball that was bigger than him. Then there was a picture of the twins in the hospital and at that moment I knew that Robbie loved me very much.

Our Lips Are Sealed

Most days when I come home, Robbie has some friends over. They are downstairs playing Atari or they are outside playing basketball or they are riding their bikes around the neighborhood pretending they are in the movie *E.T.*. Robbie has a fascination with bikes and with *E.T.*. He told me that *E.T.* was the first time he ever cried in a movie. That was last summer and that was when he was nine. Robbie is always playing with his friends here or at their houses. Chad lives around the corner. Jay lives near the golf course. The other Jay lives up the hill and he uses the path through the woods in our backyard to get to his house. Robbie and the other Jay walk to school every day. The other Jay's sister used to join them but now she's at the middle school so she goes in a different direction.

On his tenth birthday, Mom and Dad plan a surprise birthday party for Robbie. He tells me he already knows about it and not to tell anyone so I don't. I think how fun it will be to watch him pretend he didn't know there was going to be a birthday party for him after school. When after school happens and everyone arrives at our house, Robbie isn't there. His whole fourth-grade class is there, but he isn't. Mom and Dad say he will be arriving in a few minutes and that something happened at school but it's fine. I hope it isn't the same thing that happened to the twins when they played April Fool's jokes. They got in trouble and I hope Robbie didn't get in trouble on his birthday. Nobody seems to mind that Robbie is going to be late. Robbie's friends are playing *Star Wars* games in the yard and the twins are on rollerblades playing hockey in the driveway. It is a nice day for a birthday party. All we need is the birthday boy.

When Robbie arrives to his own surprise birthday party, he looks a little tired at first but before we know it, he is in the yard playing with all of the boys in his class who were invited. He is running around, laughing and happy that everyone is there. He seems happy and it makes everyone else feel happy, too. The twins keep playing street hockey and Paul Clinton our across-the-street neighbor comes over and plays street hockey with them until there is cake and ice cream and he joins everyone else for that. It is a very fun birthday party and I'm glad I'm there to help out and be the older sister.

A month before the birthday party, I go upstairs to my room and find one of my dolls has her hair cut short like a boy. I didn't do it. I wouldn't have done such a thing to one of my dolls. I don't hold scissors well, and I don't enjoy playing with my dolls' hair. What could have happened? I don't understand because it's not like when I'm away the dolls can do these things by themselves. I don't even really like having the dolls anyway. I prefer the stuffed animals because they are soft and I can squeeze them and they don't look at me and make me feel not right. I like stuffed animals because when I play with them I know it's pretend because tigers and Gund dogs and Curious Georges don't really talk. It's all pretend so it's fun. Dolls look like they can be people but they

52

are not. They look at me like they have something to say but they can't say it. So I don't really care that Mandy the doll had her hair cut short. Still, it is a mystery to me, and when Mom comes upstairs and sees me looking at Mandy the doll that looks like a boy she gets very angry.

That night in Dad's study I hear Mom and Dad talking very seriously with Robbie. They are talking in low voices through the door and the sound of their voices makes me want to not listen anymore. I don't hear Robbie at all. This makes my insides feel numb because when I think about him inside the study with the closed door and with Mom and Dad talking at him very seriously and him not saying anything it makes me want to walk away from the closed door so I don't feel any more numb on my insides. So I head to the top of the stairs and I sit there, just thinking about things that are not about Robbie listening to the low voices and not saying anything in return.

After that day, everything seems like it is normal. Robbie arrives at breakfast the next day looking like he feels like his regular self. Mom pours Dad his coffee and says something about how he needs to eat more for breakfast than just toast. He says he's gotta go so he grabs his briefcase and his lightweight spring jacket and he heads out the back door. Kenny and Danny pour a second bowl of cereal. Mom carves up a grapefruit and places it in front of Robbie, who glances at it before wolfing it down. The clock says 7:43 and I think that's about right. My van will be here in about fifteen minutes and my lunch needs to be placed in my backpack.

Mom is on the phone when I get home and she shushes me away and it tells me that she's having an important conversation. That and she stretches the phone cord around the pantry door and walks into the dining room for more privacy. I go upstairs to put away my backpack after emptying the lunchbox in the kitchen sink. On the way to my room, I pass by Robbie's bedroom and his door is open a crack and I see him through the crack in the door and he is lying on the floor talking to Sandy. He is lying on the brown rug in his bedroom talking to our dog Sandy and he is patting his face while he talks to him. He looks like he is stretching Sandy's face as he talks to him and a moment later, I notice that his eyes are red because when he sees me in the doorway he says it's all right, but his eyes are red. He is looking at me with red eyes and telling me he is all right, but don't I have to empty out my backpack from school? I think that is a good idea. I walk to my room and leave Robbie talking face to face with Sandy while Mom is downstairs talking on the phone to someone else.

The next day while I sit on the radiator waiting for Mike and the van to arrive I see Robbie walk down the driveway heading to school. I see his backpack on his back and he is wearing shorts and a collar shirt. Robbie walks quickly, which means he is excited to go to school. I understand why because he has so many friends and he is good at school. Mom and Dad are always putting his report card on the refrigerator and asking him about his day. I see him meet up with a group of kids who are also going to school. He becomes part of their pack and he looks just right.

But I don't see the other Jay with him. In fact, I didn't see the other Jay come down the path in the woods to knock on the back door to see if Robbie was ready to go to school with him yesterday either. When Robbie's tenth birthday party happens about a month later, I notice that the other Jay isn't there and that

I haven't seen him come down the path in the woods to knock on the back door to see if Robbie's ready to go to school since before Mom was on the phone and Robbie was talking with Sandy on the brown bedroom carpet with red eyes telling me he's all right.

Our House

Our house isn't little. It has many rooms upstairs and downstairs and it has a huge basement where there is a playroom and an office where Dad keeps his computer and a woodshop with power tools and a laundry room and a wine closet and a train set that is very large and runs on electricity. There is a hallway to the shop where Robbie and the twins keep their hockey equipment. The basement smells a bit like oil and gas because the water boiler and gas heater are down there but my parents say it is fine. The pipes beneath the ceiling are fine, too, they say. The stairs going down to the basement are steep, and the light string is at the bottom of the stairs, so anyone who walks down the stairs needs to walk in the dark and bat their hand in front of their face in order to find the string to pull for the light. This makes for a challenge every time I want to head downstairs, and I always turn the kitchen lights on upstairs so the top part of the stairs are lit up. In the playroom part of the basement there is a trunk we keep all of our Legos in. Underneath the stairs is the Mini Motor Mat, where my brothers play with their Matchbox cars. There are shelves with puzzles, board games, a Speak & Spell and a box of *Star Wars* figures.

There are posters on the wall, and the one that I always

remember is of a goat standing on rocks all by himself and underneath the picture is "I'm so behind, I think I'm first!" Dad told me what it says a long time ago, and I remember his hands in his pockets and him up and down on his tiptoes when he reads the poster to me and adds that the goat isn't in a bad place to be. I like seeing that poster there because not only is it a funny-looking goat but it is also a memory of Dad chuckling to himself.

The train set is important to Dad because he and Robbie built it together using tools from the woodshop and train equipment from England. The train set makes me feel peaceful because it is colorful, with small villages, and tunnels through snow-capped mountains. The trains are large and modern with a headlight in the front and a caboose in the back with a person standing on the back facing where the train came from. On the first night we use the train set, Dad calls us all downstairs. Our across-the-street neighbors, the Clintons, are over enjoying the extra daylight that happens in the early part of summer before we head to the Cape. My brothers and Paul are friends and the twins play street hockey with him and Robbie plays *Star Wars* with him. Paul rushes downstairs followed by my brothers. Dad is waiting with a dial in his hands. This dial is for the speed of the train, he says. It is to make the train go fast or slow. While he has our attention, Dad thanks Robbie and Paul for helping him put the train set together. To the sound of clapping, Robbie and Paul smile. Robbie bows. Paul can't keep his eyes off what he built.

Dad hands the dial over to Robbie and he hits the on switch. Concentrating hard on the train, Robbie starts turning the dial and the train starts to speed up. Before we know it, the train is snaking between the villages, through the tunnel, alongside the lake shore. A grin opens up on Robbie, and the crowd of people watching are silenced by the spectacle of this large and detailed train set made with such care by Dad, Robbie and Paul. I notice an unfamiliar smell becoming stronger. The best way to describe it is like the back of the television set. It isn't a burning smell like the stove or the fireplace. But my insides tell me that it is something burning.

In his excitement, Robbie allows the train to go very fast down the straightaway and he ignores the red flashing lights on the traffic crossings. The smell gets heavier and the train moves faster and the audience gets more hushed. Then comes the snap sound, and before I know it, Robbie is on the floor, like he is suddenly taking a nap but I know he isn't because his face looks gray and that isn't a good thing. The commotion that follows is horrible and busy and raw feelings of adults trying to help and kids trying to understand.

Even before Robbie returns from the hospital, Dad has taken apart the train set and put it into boxes and stored the boxes in the upper part of the garage, which means we are never going to see the train set again because anything that is put away in the upstairs part of the garage is never seen again. This is the place where rocking horses, Sit 'n' Spins, wooden baby cradles and pogo sticks disappear. In the case of Robbie and the train, Dad's decision makes a lot of sense. Sometimes it is better to tuck things away from view in order to not get a sudden attack of the sobs long after the reason for sadness has passed.

My favorite television show is *Little House on the Prairie*. It takes place a long time ago and it is about a family with three children who live in a small house in the middle of nowhere but close enough to a small town that has what every town needs, including a general store and a church that turns into a school on Sundays. The parents ride horse carriages in order to get where they need to go, and the children are all daughters who find a way to get along even when they don't. *Little House on the Prairie* is on reruns now, so I'm able to watch it every day after my van drops me off from school. It is also on Monday nights, and when I watch at that time the characters are older and every episode is new.

The main reasons I like *Little House* isn't because of what happens, even though that can be exciting, especially when Mary goes blind or there is a blizzard or the mean girl named Nellie gets consequences for her actions. The house where the family lives is small and the kitchen is the same as the living room and there is no den. The parents sleep in the room next to the kitchen and the three girls sleep upstairs where they share a bedroom. Everyone can hear each other, even when they don't want to. In the evenings sometimes the father will play his fiddle and they will all enjoy his music together. There is a dog named Jack and he is part of the family as much as everyone else. Jack reminds me of Sandy because he is always around during important family moments like when a child gets scarlet fever or the mother can't find the money she saved for Christmas presents.

The town where they all live is like the family because even though they are not related they care for each other and they protect each other. If there is an Indian raid or if there is a mean person from the big city who wants to build a train station right next to the school-church, the townspeople will come together to fight it. Any fight between kids in the schoolyard gets stopped immediately because no one is left alone to deal with their own issues. At church on Sundays, there is a sermon that is connected to the townspeople, and at school during the week, there are lessons taught by the nicest teacher imaginable.

People who want to get away from the busy energy of the small town can just walk away down dirt paths that lead to the banks of crystal rivers where you can take a fishing rod from your case and plop the bait into the water and pick up a perfectly sized fish and light a fire and cook it and eat it as a mid-afternoon snack. Or they can walk in the woods and listen to the birds in the trees and hum to themselves a song they heard Pa play on his fiddle the night before. Or they can get on horseback and in no time end up in the waving grasslands, where they can get off their horse, lay down a blanket, and take a nap with their cap over their face so they don't get sunburned. For a place that is so simple and small, there are a lot of things to do and there are a lot of nice people who support each other, even if they are in a temporary disagreement. By the end of the episode, there is a handshake and an apology and life goes on in a better way than it was going before.

This is why I don't understand why I'm watching the town explode on the television right in front of me. This is why the last episode I ever watched of *Little House* was the entire town being blown up by someone mean who did not get a consequence for his actions because it is impossible to rebuild a town after it's been blown up and have it the exact same like it wasn't ever blown up before. When I watch this episode I think about the television movie I saw recently where entire cities get blown up and that this can happen in real life so we all need to disarm now. As I watch Walnut Grove get blown up, I spot Robbie looking over at me and he tells me don't worry it's just a television show and everything is imaginary. I don't think he is right in this case because if it's just imaginary and just a television show then that means that the good people in the town don't really exist and the peaceful places to go aren't real and it means that my feelings when I watch that show might not be real either. And I know for a fact that isn't true. Not at all.

Hard to Say I'm Sorry

After so many winters freezing the driveway, we needed to get the stone walls lining it redone. Mom called the best stone fixer she could find in the Yellow Pages and she called him and he said he would come over to look at what he could do to the walls. The tipping point was when Mom backed her car too fast in the driveway after getting into an argument with Dad about Apple computers. I think Dad really wanted to buy the new one after seeing the commercial on television that showed it was the future. Mom said it's way too expensive and there isn't anything wrong with the system we have installed already. I think Dad bought the computer anyway, and that's what turned Mom's crank. So she got into her car and backed it out too quickly and as a result the stones at the end of the driveway don't look right and it bothers her every time she pulls in the driveway. It bothers me, too.

Kenny and Danny are playing street hockey when the stone fixer arrives in a light blue station wagon. He is wearing a greasy white sweatshirt and shorts even though it's not a very warm day and he has scratches on his legs that probably need to be looked at by a professional. He has black eyes and his face has deep wrinkles and the wrinkles around his eyes make them look like you can only see the black part of his eyes, not the white part around it.

I feel like it is important for me to keep my distance, so I don't stand too close when Mom introduces me. The twins might feel the same way because they didn't even stop playing street hockey when Mom introduced them. They will probably hear about this later, after the stone fixer leaves.

Robbie comes from around the side of the house and introduces himself without Mom telling him to. He is wearing gloves and removes one of them to shake the stone fixer's hand. They talk. I step closer in order to hear what they are talking about. Robbie is asked about why he's wearing gloves. He is wearing gloves because he has been cleaning out the rabbit hutch. "You have rabbits?" the stone fixer asks. Robbie replies that yes, we do have rabbits. Two of them. Would you like to see? The stone fixer must like rabbits because he says that yes, he would love to see the rabbits in the hutch around the side of the house. So we walk.

I don't remember much of what they talk about after Robbie introduces Cinnamon and Spice to the stone fixer and shows him the hutch and how clean it is. I think he is trying to impress the stone fixer and Mom, who is standing with them. The hutch does look clean right now. I think Robbie did a good job getting rid of all the rabbit poop and refilling the hay and water bottle and pellet bowl. Robbie really does not enjoy cleaning the rabbit hutch. Dad says that he is his own worst enemy because the longer he waits to clean the hutch the harder it becomes to clean. Dad seems to make Robbie more frustrated by saying this. My thoughts are drifting toward other things Robbie doesn't like to do…like weeding, doing dishes and shoveling the driveway. Yet my ears perk up when I hear the stone fixer say, "So if you ever get too tired of cleaning the hutch, let me know. I make a mean rabbit stew."

I feel a shock wave from Robbie upon hearing this. I think I make a shock wave also, because of what the stone fixer just said. Mom is out of earshot fixing one of the hanging plants on the terrace. In the silence that follows, I wish Mom had heard what the stone fixer said, but it is too late – he said it and Robbie and I heard it and from now on we agree to protect Cinnamon and Spice from the stone fixer and his beady eyes that stare at our furry little rabbits.

Dad is a teacher. He teaches at the school my brothers are going to. Every day they wear a tie and they carry bigger backpacks and sometimes hockey duffels to meet the bus at the bus stop in front of St Paul's Church down the street. When they meet the bus there at 7:25 every day, Dad opens the door and they get inside. Dad also drives the school bus. He had to get a special bus driver's license and he had to take a big test. Now he leaves the house before everyone wakes up and he gets the bus ready to pick everyone up for school. He drives his red Volvo to pick up the yellow bus every morning. His red Volvo has a plastic Stanley Cup trophy hanging from the sunroof. It dangles from the sunroof handle and it reminds Dad how good it felt when the Bruins won the Stanley Cup.

I don't have breakfast with my brothers anymore because they get to school earlier than I do. My van still picks me up at 8:00 but my brothers leave the house at 7:20. When I head downstairs for breakfast, it's just me and Sandy and then Mom comes home from dropping my brothers off at St Paul's Church and she pours a cup of coffee and stands leaning on the counter sipping her coffee and looking out for red cardinals at the bird feeder. It is a quiet way to start the day and I feel relaxed. It takes a while for

64

my tiredness to go away. The van ride with Mike makes sure I'm wide awake when I get to school, especially when there are not many commercials on the radio.

Dad doesn't like to grade papers in his study. He says it makes him feel bored after a long day of bus driving and teaching and coaching sports in the afternoon. So instead he will bring a stack of papers with him while he watches the news on television. On special nights, we join him in the den to watch the news on television. Mom will make something easy like hamburgers or TV dinners or mac and cheese and we will unfold the TV trays and sit in front of the television and watch the news or whatever other thing Dad wants us to watch together.

Once Danny made Mom upset when he said he likes the food better when we eat in front of the television than the food we normally have for dinner. It made Mom upset because she said she doesn't put any effort into the food we eat in front of the television and saying that really hurts her feelings. Danny got up, walked over and gave Mom a big hug with his wide smile and said he didn't mean it like that. Mom seemed to melt at that moment and we could all see that things were better. Still, I think we all agree with Danny about the food, even though we would never tell her that after seeing how it made her feel.

Tonight we are watching news about gorillas in Central America. The gorillas are fighting in a war in Central America and they are killing a lot of people. I don't understand how gorillas end up fighting people and why they think that's a good idea. People have guns and other things that protect them. Gorillas are stronger and they know how to live in the jungle if the people chase them that way. But they don't do anything in the jungle that matters to people in Central America, do they?

The news ends with a nice report about Prince Charles and Lady Diana who are coming to visit President Reagan in Washington and will then go to California for vacation. I remember all of us in Mom and Dad's bedroom early in the morning watching their wedding that took place in a beautiful church in London. I remember the chariot, the horses, her long wedding dress and them all waving from the balcony of the palace. I remember looking up at Mom and seeing tears in her eyes after Charles and Diana said their vows. I remember looking at my brothers, who were all glued to the television. It was magical in the palace and it felt nice in the bedroom watching the magic on the television.

This memory is interrupted by a screeching sound outside. Dad jumps out of his seat, knocking over his pile of papers, and runs to the window to check on the commotion. Robbie and the twins follow him and as they get to the window, Dad is already outside. I hear him opening the gate to the pen and I all of a sudden know exactly what is going on. I think Robbie does, too, because he looks down and gets very quiet and leaves the den. The twins stay staring out the window. A commercial for WD-40 plays on the television and it is loud.

The day after Cinnamon was taken by the raccoon, Mom tells us at dinner that she will sell Spice to the stone fixer because he expressed interest in having a new rabbit. Robbie asks if she needs to be reminded that he will make Spice into rabbit stew but Mom looks at him in a way that causes Robbie to be quiet for the rest of the dinner. He doesn't eat much tonight, and he doesn't talk much for a few more days. If he hadn't met the stone fixer, he would not have gotten quiet for days. If he hadn't left the rabbit hutch open by accident, that would have probably made him not get quiet either. I want to tell Robbie that accidents happen and that he should be proud of how he kept such good care of the rabbits he didn't like taking care of. But I know that it wouldn't come out right because it would have felt funny when everyone knows he was being irresponsible like he is with things he doesn't like to do such as weeding, doing the dishes and shoveling the driveway. Mom and Dad say Robbie has been more irresponsible lately and I agree because it's true. Maybe it has to do with him getting older like me or school or something about the weather.

Come Sail Away

The Cape house is old. The floors creak and make snapping sounds in the middle of the night. When we're on the porch in the evening, the screen door opens and slams with the breeze. This is why the house makes me dizzy. The windows have glass that is bent so sometimes the trees outside are magnified and sometimes they are made small depending on where I stand when I look through them. The floorboards are curved and have dips and bumps. Gammy jokes that the dining room table makes her taller or shorter because of which side she sits on. The twins got in trouble once for rolling tennis balls down the dining room floor because it is so slanted and Gammy and Grandpops might slip on them. The stairs are even steeper than at Granny's house. I grip the banister tightly and my palms sweat at night. Going up stairs is easier than down stairs. When you go up stairs, you only look at what's up in front of you. You don't know how high you've climbed. When you go down stairs, you only see how far down you have to go. For someone like me, it creates a dizzy feeling that makes me wish I could sleep downstairs somewhere instead of where I always sleep.

We call the Cape house 'Tide River'. This is because it is on a river and there are tides. The tides make the river fill up so it almost looks like a lake. Even if you can't see this, you know the tide is high because the ramp on the dock is like a bridge. It is flat across so I can easily walk from the wooden part across the ramp-bridge to the rubber float on the other side. When it is low tide, the ramp-bridge is very steep and I get the dizzy feeling again. Also, I grip the side of the ramp-bridge posts and I see the fiddler crabs in the mud below. Sometimes I see a blue claw, and it gives me a chill because blue-claw crabs are huge and they have blue claws that can squeeze your toes if you're not careful. Many times I need someone to help me get down the ramp-bridge on the dock at low tide. Sometimes I just decide not to go, even if it means saying no to a boat ride on the ocean. Sometimes saying no to a boat ride is a good idea because I can stay inside and make my lists on my blank pad of paper and I can relax and not hear the funny sounds or get dizzy because being on the water makes me dizzy, too.

One morning, I wake up and I know it is going to be a beautiful day. Still in bed, I feel the warm sunlight through the shade that is lit up in yellow. I lift the shade and peek outside and see the twins following Dad who is carrying garbage bins to his car. It must be a dump day. They follow him to the car and Sandy suddenly runs across the yard and onto the gravel driveway where he grabs the tennis ball with his mouth, skids and turns completely around and heads back toward the front door. The tennis ball zooms across the yard again, followed by Sandy, who grabs it again with his mouth and runs back to whoever is throwing it. It must be Robbie, because the twins are with Dad and Mom doesn't throw to the dog and Gammy and Grandpops wouldn't be throwing either because I don't think they throw balls anymore. Dad's red

Volvo heads down the driveway with the gray trailer behind it carrying three big garbage bins with the covers on each of them except the one carrying tree branches.

I'm finishing up my pancakes with sticky real Vermont maple syrup. I'm eating at the kids' table in the playroom, which is really good because the real Vermont maple syrup is sticky and there is a plastic tablecloth that can handle the sticky real Vermont maple syrup. The twins run into the playroom where I'm eating and Danny says, "Come on, Claire! We're going on *Windsong*!" I don't know how I feel about this because going on *Windsong* means a whole lot of things. It means getting organized. I need to pack a bag that has a sweatshirt, suntan lotion, sunglasses, a hat, a towel, and other stuff I can't think of right now because I'm still eating my pancakes. But I feel a growing excitement about going on *Windsong* today because it is such a beautiful day and who wouldn't want to spend such a beautiful day on the ocean on a sailboat?

Mom enters the playroom with my green bag in one hand and my yellow lifejacket in the other. She tells me we are all set to go and that I need to get to the dock. I ask about putting on a bathing suit because this sailing day has come up as a bit of a surprise but she tells me it's not a swimming kind of day and that we really need to get going. *All right, I'm ready to go.* But first she takes my suntan lotion from my green bag and she spends an eternity covering my whole arms, legs, face and neck and ears and behind the ears with that cold and greasy stuff. As if the real Vermont maple syrup didn't feel sticky enough.

The sun is high in the sky and we are flattened out on the ocean and the wind is soft and the air smells like salt and the sound of ropes beating against the sail and the side of the boat becomes musical to my ears. The twins sit up on the top of the cabin and Robbie is in the very front of the boat, sitting with legs on both sides of the wooden part that shoots out from the bow of the boat. He holds the wire in front of him with both hands while we sail toward the sandy land in front of us. A plane flies overhead, buzzing with the sound of its propeller and trailing a long sign with red letters that advertise something I can't read but it's all right because it's just an advertisement and Dad says we sail in order to get away from stuff like that.

I'm munching on salt and vinegar Cape Cod Potato Chips and there is a Diet Coke with my name on it in the big blue cooler that also has bologna and cheese sandwiches wrapped in baggies and more chips and soda and seedless green grapes and beer for Dad. Eating on the boat is one of my favorite things about *Windsong*. Except when the weather isn't a beautiful sunny day. When the boat tips and everyone gets wet, it isn't fun to eat on the boat at all.

I look over at Dad, who is at the helm of the boat, which means he is steering the wheel and looking ahead of him for things to aim for. He is always pointing out these things to me: buoys, lighthouses, TV towers and other things that are good markers. Dad never looks as calm and content as he does when he is on *Windsong*. Mom and Dad bought *Windsong* from Granny and Grandy five years ago when I was eight. Dad thinks it's the best thing he's ever bought – even better than the Apple computer. Mom agrees and says yes even though it gives her a headache. I don't think she gets a headache when we are sailing, though.

The sun above our heads seems to make time slow down and speed up all the same. While we sail, it seems like we are going very slowly and that time is just tick-tick-ticking along like molasses (or real Vermont maple syrup). But when I look at my watch, I always want to tap it to make sure it is telling the right time. It's always later in the day than I think it is, and I think that's because something happens to time when we are on the water. Time flies when you're having fun, but it's not as simple as that on *Windsong*. There is something else about time and water and salt air and birds all around us that makes time play special tricks on us. I think it's part of why Dad likes sailing on *Windsong* as much as he does.

I'm awoken from my deep sleep by Robbie, who has moved from the front of the boat to the helm. He and Dad are at the wheel together, and Dad asks if Robbie would like to take the helm by himself. Robbie is an excellent sailor, even if he is only ten years old. He has won so many trophies and plates and medals for sailing that they fill three shelves in his bedroom at home. He doesn't brag about it. Instead, he just keeps sailing and going to the yacht club every day to keep getting better. Dad is proud of Robbie and sailing, and he wants Robbie to love sailing as much as he did when he was Robbie's age.

I know this because it's what Mom told Gammy one time on the porch when they were watching Robbie sail the Sailfish on the river at high tide and he was flipping it over and every time he flipped it over Grandpops would wonder whether Robbie knew how to sail at all. It always bothered Grandpops when Robbie would not treat boats with respect by flipping them over all the time in the river in front of all the other people who have houses on the river. Based on the smile and laughter Robbie expressed when flipping the Sailfish over, I thought that it's not that he doesn't respect sailing. It's that he knows how to sail so well that he becomes playful like the gorillas swinging in the jungle

72

in Central America. I love seeing Robbie that happy, even if it makes Grandpops wonder whether he respects sailing as much as he thinks he should.

To put a lid on it, one night Dad made a toast to Robbie at the dining room table. We were invited to come in for the toasts, and Dad's toast to Robbie was because Robbie won the seamanship award at the yacht club. The seamanship award was for more than just sailing. It was about respect for the sea, Dad said. It was given to the person who best understood what it means to be a sailor in all senses of the word. While Dad was talking, I looked at Robbie, who was smiling and red-faced but not because he was embarrassed. Grandpops was looking down at his napkin while Dad was talking, and when we all clinked glasses, Grandpops didn't smile and instead he closed his mouth tight so there were wrinkles on his lips. His eyes were not smiling, either, so I'm sure it's not because of something he ate.

Later that night, I could hear Dad and Grandpops talking on the porch while having a nightcap. Dad's voice was loud when talking to his father, and his father's voice was loud when talking to Dad. They got louder and louder and Robbie's name was part of their nightcap. Suddenly, they were silent. No more words and no more getting louder. I could hear one of them still on the porch because I could hear every time he put his cocktail glass down on the table. Moments later, I could hear footsteps trudging up the stairs on the other side of the house. I knew it was Grandpops because after he went up the stairs I didn't hear the footsteps anymore and his bedroom was down on that end of the house.

I wanted to go downstairs and see Dad on the porch with his nightcap but then decided to stay in bed because it was warm and I didn't want to get dizzy going down the stairs at night with my sweaty palms and I thought that Dad would rather be alone because of the conversation he had had with his father.

The next night, Grandpops made a toast to Robbie for the way he has grown as a sailor since he first started many years ago. He said that sailing is never clean because you're at the mercy of Mother Nature and she needs to be understood with sensitivity. But Robbie does a very good job of being sensitive, and this makes Grandpops believe he will continue to be an excellent sailor, like his father and his grandfather.

London Calling

I love London. It feels like a cushion there. It is a soft city. People talk softer. They walk softer. Shoes make softer sounds and leaves rustle more softly in the park. Flowers bloom softer and cars drive more softly around corners. The voice on the Tube is softer than on the T and the signs are written in a softer handwriting that is pleasing to my eye. The colors are softer and the sky is a softer blue when the sun is out. The language is softer in London and in England. There is a softer accent that sounds more like a song. The birds chirp in a wider range of songs and the dogs bark more softly. I like the softness of London as much as I like the people there. When Granny one time lost her umbrella by leaving it at The Ritz after tea, a stranger offered her his even though it was raining cats and dogs. I don't understand that expression but I giggle when I hear it, especially when I use it. A lot of people complain about London weather but I don't mind that, either. Even when it rains cats and dogs, people are still nice, the Tube lady still gently suggests that we mind the gap, and the nice taxi driver still tells us all about the history of the Sex Pistols (not a bad word because it's the name of a rock band).

This is funny because London should make me dizzy. They drive on the other side of the road. We look right first, then left when crossing the street. We walk on the left side and we are careful to stand on the right when we are on escalators. Escalators still make me dizzy in London, and that is because of my challenges with heights. London should make me dizzy because they use different coins that I don't recognize and there are a million people in a small place. It should make me dizzy because the buildings are from a hundred years ago and so are some of the cars and some of the outfits like the guards at Buckingham Palace. London should make me dizzy because they still have a queen and sometimes a king and other royal people and changing of the guard. London should make me dizzy because of all the big airplanes that fly over the river of the city and the words people use like "mate", "Marmite" and "sorry" instead of "excuse me". Using sorry is another reason London is softer. Sorry is a soft and warm word. It's the first word I think about when I think about London. Sorry and "cheers", which always makes me smile when I hear it.

The biggest reason I love London is because of Juliet. She's not really from London but she's from England and it is Juliet who introduced me to London and the soft way people live there. Even though we are a long airplane ride apart, Juliet is my very best friend. Robbie once called Juliet my "Sister from Another Mister" and Mom got very, very upset at him because it's not true and because he said it in front of the twins. I don't understand what Robbie meant and I don't understand why Mom got so upset by what Robbie meant but I do know that when anyone says anything bad in front of the twins then they should get yelled at because they are young. And I also know that if I had to have a sister, I would want her to be Juliet.

Juliet is like England because she is quieter than where I am

76

from where the cars are honking and everyone talks loudly. I'm not trying to sound like a complainer but it's true, especially when you grow up with brothers. Brothers yell at each other a lot. I think when Juliet visits they try to not yell as much and they also take their yelling outside. But Juliet doesn't yell at all. She barely talks. When she does, it is in a really quiet voice that gets people like Mom to lean forward and ask, "What did you just say?" and then she repeats it without skipping a beat. And without raising the volume.

Juliet makes me think of a mirror. She and I are like when you look in a mirror and you see yourself. But it's not yourself because it's your right hand waving back at your left hand. And it's your left eye that winks at the right eye of the reflected person. Juliet is my reflection because she does everything I do. She doesn't speak much at all but I know what she is thinking and she is thinking about me and our friendship and it feels solid and reliable. Like a mirror image. She doesn't cause a commotion ever. But she is always there, silently, and speaking a thousand thoughts in a way that I can truly understand.

Juliet's and my favorite place to be is the screen porch at the Cape house painting seashells. From there, we can watch Robbie flipping the Sailfish over and over again. We can watch the twins and our neighbor Larry go fishing at the end of the dock. We can watch Dad and Grandpops fixing the engine on the whaler. We see these things and we hear the noise. But that doesn't distract us from painting our seashells with watercolor paint from Crayola. My favorite shell to paint is a scallop because I like how the colors get dark in the creases. Juliet's favorite shell to paint is a clam because it's the biggest and she likes its smooth surface.

Gammy is usually sitting on the other side of the porch from us, listening to her staticky Cape Cod Classical radio station and doing needlepoint. When she's really relaxed, Gammy will hum along with the song being played. "Dyah dyah da-da-da... dyum DYUM...dyum...DYUM..." When she's really relaxed, her eyes glisten and she focuses so much on the needlepoint it is like she is not on the porch with us or with anyone anywhere. Gammy taught my brothers how to golf by swinging their golf clubs to the sound of her favorite song, 'The Blue Danube'. "Dyah dyah da-da-da...dyum DYUM...dyum DYUM..."

Juliet keeps me company on the Cape because Kenny and Danny have each other and Robbie has his yacht club friends. She is a good friend because she can be with me for anything and it is like having company that wants to be there but doesn't have to broadcast it to everyone. Juliet doesn't broadcast much at all. She is silent most of the time. Her eyes are wide open, and she sees everything. I know this because she's silent on the outside but talkative to me without using her mouth. Juliet and I talk to each other without using our mouths. We don't need to. She understands what I'm saying and I understand what she's saying without talking using words. I have never had a friend like that before.

The only thing that comes close to this kind of friendship is Kenny and Danny. They also talk to each other and they share the same thoughts. I know this because one time Danny ran into my room and, before saying why he was running into my room, he looked and said, "Your calendar is on the wrong month." He didn't do anything about it, though. An hour later, Kenny ran into my room and before saying why he was running into my room he looked and said, "Your calendar is on the wrong month." Kenny, being Kenny, fixed it immediately, which made me very happy because calendars are like clocks when they don't match up to the right date and time. Another example is when Kenny got three stitches above his right eye from falling off the swing. A week later, Danny got three stitches above his right eye from getting a hockey stick in it. That example might just be coincidence. But the calendar example isn't, and there are many more where that came from when the twins say the same things at different times.

I think it is fascinating. And I also think I'm lucky to feel that way with Juliet. I think Mom thinks it is lucky that Juliet is my friend because she has said before that she can leave us for hours and not have to worry. She is right about not having to worry because Juliet is the most thoughtful and safe friend I have. She moves slowly and she thinks before she acts. She is quiet and she doesn't make anyone upset at her. I think we are a perfect friendship because we don't make a lot of noise and we are peaceful. Plus, she has the London accent that makes anything she says sound soft and kind and good. Juliet's accent is just right for her, just like Granny's accent is just right, too.

I watch as my big, flowery luggage bag goes up the ramp and then on to the bigger ramp and then under the strips of black cloth that make it disappear. The noisiness and the crowds usually make me feel dizzy, but tonight I don't feel dizzy one bit. Mom and Dad guide me up the escalator and walk with me through the security check. Dad holds my ticket and shows it to the officer who waves the three of us through. We are greeted at Gate 42 by a friendly woman with a long, blond braid down her back and a navy-blue triangle hat with a red stripe on the side.

Imogen said she would be my guide for the entire flight. She spoke in a soft London accent and I then knew I wouldn't get dizzy at all on the plane.

The flight was not very interesting because it was at night and I tried to sleep but had a not very good time doing it so there's nothing much to report. At one point, the nice lady with the soft London accent knelt down in the aisle and talked with me for so long I can't believe her knees still work. We talked about all sorts of things like Paddington Bear, marmalade, Wimbledon and Queen Elizabeth. Imogen seemed particularly impressed when I told her about Charles and Diana. I think she thinks that because I'm an American I won't know anything about England. But if you grew up with a Granny who sounds like the Queen, you would learn a lot about England. I don't know how, because I don't ever remember having a lesson, but you would.

The first thing Juliet's father did when he picked me up from the airport was apologize for making me fly "British Awful". I started telling him how it wasn't bad at all and that I actually enjoyed the flight a lot. But his voice is so deep and powerful I knew that I wouldn't be able to really say what I wanted to say. Not that he didn't want to listen to me, it's just that sometimes when you talk with someone who has a loud voice it's not only because they want their words to be heard. So I stay quiet, nod, watch the emerald-green pastures blur past my fancy-car window, and sense the excitement mounting in my tummy that I will soon be with Juliet again.

Like the emerald-green pastures past my fancy-car window, my week with Juliet is a blur. It is cloth napkins and tulips at the table. It is *The Sound of Music* and dining with the woman who played Maria afterwards. It is a horse carriage through a tree-lined park in central London followed by high tea in shiny silver. It is swimming in the pool behind Juliet's house and walking into her village pub while her father entertains everyone with exciting stories as his face gets red. It is learning how to stand up straight from her mother, who reminds me of Granny because she, too, looks like a queen.

Yet my week with Juliet is also time spent coloring together at the table, sitting side by side. It is eating scones with clotted cream and marmalade. It is doing a puzzle with big pieces while listening to records from musicals like *Mary Poppins*. It is walking on the pathways behind her house and through where the cows and horses are kept. It is tucking in for bed and then turning off the light and then quietly talking for a long time. It is giggling at silly thoughts and funny faces, and trying to hold in our laughter at church on Sunday. My week with Juliet is about all of those things and so many more that I can't keep them inside all at once so some come out as tears on my plane ride back to Boston.

Careless Whisper

Life is busy and taking time to myself is important. My family is rushing around doing whatever they do that makes them feel right. Sometimes I think Sandy is in danger because he can get tripped on when our family is in a hurry. But Sandy is strong and flexible. I saw him once chase after a Frisbee Robbie threw in his direction but he was on a leash tied to the tree. So off Sandy goes, off after the Frisbee, and he is almost there when he suddenly does a somersault that doesn't break his neck. We are amazed he did not break his neck because Dad said the leash doesn't have any give. What it did give him was a sore neck, and we could tell because it was a long time before Sandy chased after Frisbees the way he used to. He is back to his regular self now, and it is nice to see that he isn't afraid to chase things because of the leash being tied to the tree. I think Robbie learned a lesson about taking a moment before just throwing something.

Mom works as a secretary at our church. The church is congregational, which means that it is focused on the people who go there. This is good because Mom is also focused on the people who go there. Not only because she's the church secretary, but also because when we are sitting at church she's always looking around to see the people who go there. She recognizes friends and smiles and waves. Sometimes if the service hasn't begun yet she will get up and rush over to talk to someone seated in the aisles. Mom glows in church. It is her place of congregation. That is why the church is perfect for her because it is congregational.

The name of our church is Village Church. Our town isn't a village, but I think that this is the image our church is trying to express. Our church makes our large town feel like a village. When you enter the doors and sit with the other people in the congregation and you listen to Mr. Gallagher be a minister with the other people, then our town can feel like a village, like we are small enough to fit under one roof and it feels warm and supportive not just because of the building being made out of bricks, but because the people there are strong with each other. There are babies and old people. There are sick people and people with other troubles who are looking for a village to help support them. There are people who don't have serious troubles and are not sick but they have questions. You can see who these people are because their questions are on their faces. They have eyes that are like question marks and they have foreheads with deep wrinkles and they walk with a curve in their back that makes them seem shorter because they are carrying so many questions in their heads that their heads are heavy and their bodies are bent.

I have questions sometimes but they never stick to me and make my head heavy. They have answers and they don't lead to more questions like I think happens to people when they have so many questions in their heads. Their questions lead to more questions, which lead to more questions and the list goes on and on. What questions do is they make me impulsive like Robbie can get. When a question gets in my head, I ask it. If nobody is listening, I will ask the question again, the same way. I will rinse, lather and repeat this until I get an answer, even if it is "I don't *know!*" I don't try to be annoying when I have a question, but it tingles in my brain like there are hairs inside my head until the question is answered, even if it is "I don't *know!*" Maybe this is why my head isn't heavy with questions because when one pops in, I get someone to answer it quickly, so there is no traffic jam of questions building up in my brain.

Mr. Gallagher is our minister and he looks at me with clear eyes and a smile that curls up on the sides of his mouth. His height is bigger than Dad's. He greets me with a "Hello, Claire. I'm glad you're here with us." I surprise myself by giving him a hug. He is the safest person to hug not in my family and not Juliet. I hug him and I don't let go until he gently with warm hands releases himself from my hug and he still holds my hands with his warm hands and looks at me with his clear eyes and his curling mouth and he says, "I think you're ready to be confirmed." I find myself nodding and he moves one hand to my shoulder and he walks with me to an empty fold-up seat and I sit down like the other fourteen-year-olds who are here to get ready for confirmation.

Confirmation Sunday isn't a big deal for me because we rehearsed a lot beforehand and also because when I stand up there with the other fourteen-year-olds I look out at the village of people who are smiling and looking warmly at me. This feels good down to my heart and I have no questions. I know that this is a big deal because everyone gets a Bible and they are told to use it. Even though I can't read in my Bible, Mr. Gallagher gives me one with all sorts of pictures of Jesus, Mary, the cross, camels, shepherds and halos. If Mr. Gallagher were in my Bible, he would have a halo because he shines light and he has the clear eyes that show answers not questions.

After the service at Village Church, I return home to a picnic outside in the back yard with a lot of family friends and relatives. Before I head outside with everyone else, I go upstairs to my room and place my new Bible on my dresser, between the old silver brush and the hand mirror. I like the idea of seeing my Bible every time I go to the dresser to take out clothes for the next day. I place it in the middle of the dresser so I can see it every day. If I have time, I can open it and look at the pictures and make up stories and find out answers to questions I don't even know I have.

Outside, I see my cousin Rachel who is my closest cousin because she has a wonderful imagination and she likes to pretend-play tea party with me and my stuffed animals. Rachel and I have done many projects together and we have had sleepovers and we have gone to *The Nutcracker* with Granny and had tea afterwards at the Four Seasons overlooking Boston Garden. Rachel is five years younger than me so she's the twins' age. But she and I have always thought the same and talked the same and played the same together.

I walk over to Rachel and tell her I like her hair and I hold her hands like Mr. Gallagher held mine and I tell her, *I'm so glad you're here.* Rachel looks from side to side and her hands twitch and her feet shift underneath her pretty flower dress. She looks around and then says that she needs to go play with my brothers. She wants to play with my brothers. She looks at me with her big brown eyes and she whispers, "I think I've outgrown you." I think she says sorry before she quickly walks away. I'm left with a new question in my head but I'm afraid to ask it because if I do ask it I might not get the only answer I want. If I ask this question,

I might not get the answer that she didn't mean it and that she will return and that we will continue like we were. If that isn't the answer then it isn't worth asking the question because it is why sometimes asking questions can make us heavy and sad and walking with a curve in our back like our heads are too heavy for our bodies...or our hearts are too weak for our heads.

Run to You

The school my brothers go to and that Dad drives a bus for and teaches at is on a hill and it looks like it belongs somewhere else and not near Boston. This is because it has red tile roofs that you don't see anywhere else except when I went to England to visit Juliet and we flew to an island that was warm and had a lot of rocks before getting to the soft and sandy beaches below. The water there was a color blue that was purple in some areas, and the people wore small bathing suits except for Juliet and me. The roofs there were orange and the buildings fitted in there better than the buildings at the school my brothers go to and that Dad drives a bus for and teaches at.

Everyone is out today. All of the kids are wearing purple or gray uniforms and white shorts. My brothers are out there and I know they wear gray because that's the color of their uniforms all the time and when Mom washes them it is always her washing gray T-shirts and sweatshirts and sweatpants for the colder weather. Dad is out there, too, and he wears a whistle around his neck that bounces off his purple windbreaker. I can't see him that well because there are other teachers there who are dressed the same way wearing the same baseball hats and windbreakers. I stand with Mom on a set of bleachers in order to watch my brothers compete and we are in a crowd of people dressed all the same: the moms wear bright springtime dresses and the dads wear navy suits and ties because they are coming from their offices to be here for Field Day at the school my brothers go to and that Dad drives a bus for and teaches at.

I see Robbie and he is concentrating hard while he stands in front of the number "4" on the track. He jumps up and down and does some quick leg stretches and he looks at the ground most of the time. He wears a black T-shirt and white shorts and his blond hair is beginning to darken because he is in eighth grade now and his hair will get darker and his legs will grow because that's what Dad told him is going to happen because it happened to him around the same age. Robbie is joined by five other eighth graders and two of them also wear black and three of them wear red. It is the blacks against the reds, I keep hearing. And I see a huge scoreboard at the end of the football field that is now the Field Day field. The scoreboard reads: Blacks – 57 Reds – 43. Maybe Robbie can help the Black team get more points when he runs quickly.

The horn squeals and off they go. I keep my eyes on Robbie as best I can even though standing on the bleachers makes me dizzy so I hold on to Mom's arm for balance. As the group of runners begins to spread out, I can see Robbie more easily. His legs really are growing because he isn't the shortest person in the group like he used to be. This makes me feel happy for him and it is because he will be changing into a man and he is ready, I think. As his long legs speed up, he begins to run faster on the long straight part of the track. He passes the person in second place so now he is only behind a very tall runner whose brown hair is like a flag on the back of his head thanks to the wind he is creating by the running.

As they round the other end of the track and begin heading for the finish line, I'm surprised to feel the butterflies in my tummy.

I calm myself by remembering that no matter how he places, he has become known as a good athlete. This is a very different feeling than how I felt when a few years ago I saw him shoot a basketball into his own team's net. It was an important game and I remember feeling confused when I saw him run to the net closest to us and nobody followed him. It didn't look right to have him break away with the ball and shoot on the net with nobody chasing him from the other team. People just stood there and watched, and the whole gym became eerily quiet, like a blanket had fallen in the entire building.

After shooting the basketball into his own basket, Robbie was pulled aside by the coach and sat on the bench for the rest of the game. I think that was the hardest part, being on the bench for everyone to look at for the rest of the game knowing that he was not playing anymore because he put the ball in the wrong net. His face never got back to its normal color until we got home after the quietest car ride in memory. It didn't even matter that the radio was on.

But look at Robbie now! Running so fast with growing legs against a runner whose legs have already grown. He crosses the finish line in second place and he grins a silvery smile through his year-old braces. He will get a medal later on and when he does, I hope he wears it all the way home in the loudest car ride in memory when it doesn't even matter that the radio is off.

My turn to run comes a month later when I head to Quincy to the Special Olympics. I have done three Special Olympics and every time it is fun because all of the people who participate are helpful and nice and the athletes like me are there for the fun of it all. My favorite events are the sprint and the ball toss. The ball toss is cancelled today, so I'm only running the sprint. That's okay. I would rather run anyway because it's fun to hear the cheering at the finish line. You don't get that when you're throwing the ball.

It is such a sunny day. There are puffy white clouds in the sky and I can feel it when they get in the way of the sun because it gets cool very quickly. Everyone is wearing different colored shirts and there are balloons and streamers and cotton candy and all sorts of paper programs and schedules and notes for the people with the microphones. There are whistles and horns going off everywhere but I'm not dizzy today because I know where I'm supposed to be because I have Vicki with me and she leads the way. Actually, it is Vicki and Paula who are with me. Paula is the woman who blocked my sun at Lake Waban when I was younger. She is the one who asked me to join their circle and she called me "sister". Now Paula is here with Vicki and helping me get to where I need to go.

There are a bunch of other runners who I will be running with. They are people I recognize and also strangers. Many seem excited but some are acting in different ways. There is a boy crying at the starting line. There is another boy who is giggling while he stretches and I think he is just nervous. There is a girl who is being talked to by her mom about keeping her shoes tied. I look at my Velcro shoes and I'm happy we found a pair that will help me run faster. I look up and that's when I first see a boy who is getting into an angry argument with his father. His child-like face is red with frustration and his sky-blue eyes are welled with tears he is working hard to hide. He is wearing purple shorts and a special green color shirt that reminds me of Treasure Cay in the

Bahamas. His hair is light-colored and reddish. His intensity is felt by all of us, and I think by me especially.

I shake my head away from being caught staring at the boy throwing the temper tantrum and Vicki tells me I'm great and Paula pats me on the shoulder and I'm ready to run and to do my best and to maybe get a medal. But just maybe because I don't really need it in order to have fun on this beautiful sunny day with puffy clouds and cool shadows.

I'm running harder than I've ever run before because I remember watching Robbie at his race and I think I can do the same as he did. I have always had a balance issue, like when I'm walking down the stairs and how it makes me feel dizzy with my steps. So when I see the girl in front of me fall to the ground, my first thought is how I'm surprised it is her and not me. When I ask her if she's all right, I can't understand her answer because she's crying and it is hard to be understood when you're crying. I look at her scraped-up knees and tell her I'm sorry about her knees. She looks up at my eyes and she says something like thank you. Or maybe she was saying it hurts. But whatever she said, she's crying less and she's even leaning on me to try to get up. A bunch of adults have run over by now, and one carries a medical toolbox that reminds me of my Dad's fishing box. One of the adults tells me they are restarting the race because of the accident. Before I head back to the starting line for a second time, I ask the girl what her name is. I can understand her answer perfectly. Her name is Kate.

In Doris, I sit in the front seat with Vicki driving and Paula in the back seat. Even though she's wearing sunglasses, Paula is asleep. Vicki asks if I mind if she has a cigarette "because I've been so good today with all those healthy athletes". I nod yes and she reaches for her Virginia Slims, presses in the lighter button, and rolls down the window with her strong left arm like she's done all of this a thousand times before. I look down at the medal I'm holding and it is gold and it shines with pride and it feels heavy but in a good way, like the heaviness is a reminder that I won a race today. It isn't about winning, but I do feel light and happier inside so when Vicki asks if it's okay for her to have a second cigarette, I nod and say yes again and without even skipping a beat.

Something made me run fast today and it's not only because I was thinking about Robbie and his race from a month ago. I wanted to run fast for my new friend Kate who I found out lives in Lexington, which isn't too far away from my house. She did not deserve to get hurt on such a colorful day with blue sky and puffy clouds with cool shadows. The medical adult helping her was yelling at her because he couldn't understand what she was saying. I had challenges understanding her at first, but (as I wanted to tell him but didn't) if you wait and open your ears and listen with your eyes then she becomes easy to understand. I find that when people have a hard time understanding someone they speak loudly themselves and it doesn't help. Kate said she'd like to get together sometime, and Vicki wrote down her name, address and phone number from her mom.

Something I won't even tell Vicki is that when I was running the race I realized that when I thought about the boy having a temper tantrum I ran faster. I wanted to run with all of my strength because I felt like I was being fueled by a different type of energy that came only from him. After the race, I looked for him and could not find him. I spend the rest of the car ride in Doris thinking about how I could find out what his name is.

I wanted to thank him for making me run faster. I wanted to tell him he helped me with the gold medal. I wanted to see his squinting eyes and listen to his defiant voice up close in those purple shorts and green shirt that makes me think of Treasure Cay in the Bahamas.

Later in the summer, I'm watching the real Olympics that are happening in LA and brought to us by NBC. The real Olympics are a big deal. There are huge stadiums that are filled with a million people, it looks like. The big torch is above the stadium and its fire is lit all day for the whole time the real Olympics is going on. I watch the race that made me think of my race and Robbie's race from earlier this spring. I watch as the American woman with honey blond hair is running against a barefoot woman with short dark hair like Dorothy from the Winter Olympics from a few years ago. The American woman is running ahead of the barefoot runner. She is working so hard and I wonder whether she's thinking about her own Jed, which is the name of the boy with the temper tantrum. Jed called me one night out of the blue because somehow he got my phone number and we talked and I tingled inside the whole time and now I can't wait to get together with him sometime soon. So I'm watching the American woman running and the barefoot runner is close behind her and then like lightning the American woman trips and falls and the barefoot runner continues running ahead. She doesn't stop to help the American runner and she doesn't slow down even though she knows what happened because she turned her head quickly in the accident's direction. I think the real Olympics are different than the Special Olympics because there are so many people watching it on television and in the crowded stadium. I think the barefoot runner was feeling like she needed to continue running even though the American woman was rolling on her back holding her foot and crying loudly because it's not just her hip that is deeply hurt.

When Doves Cry

Granny and Grandy spend most of their time in boats or on skis even though they live in a small house on a big hill with shiny and delicate things inside. On Wednesday nights when I'm trying to sleep I hear deep croaking bursts from the pond nobody swims in at the bottom of the hill. One night I hear a sound that makes me think about the night Cinnamon disappeared and we sold Spice to the stone fixer who made him into rabbit stew. I roll over and press the pillow closer to my head and think about the cartoon movie about the deer and the bunny and the bear that sang that silly song. When I think about colorful cartoons I get happy because colors are brighter than real life and the animals move around more like they are dancing than just moving. When animals talk it makes me feel good because there is no confusion about what they want to say. Cartoons are fun to think about when you try to fall asleep especially after you hear a scary noise coming from the bottom of the hill in the darkness outside.

Tonight Granny is preparing dinner made out of leftovers that come from rusty cans in the pantry that were taken from their boat up in Maine. Every fall we have dinners made from food from the boat and sometimes they are tasty. Tonight is scrapple. Scrapple is canned hash mixed with bacon from the refrigerator that was yesterday's breakfast. We have Heinz ketchup from the boat and canned beans that taste like metal and salt and butter. Before dinner we have cheese and crackers and each have green spots on them the color of olives like in Grandy's cocktail. I have learned by now to close my eyes and chew quickly.

Dinner with them is usually Granny talking and Grandy listening. She usually talks about her friends. Grandy always asks, "Who?", and Granny speaks louder to remind him of her friends and their names and how the last time he saw them was only a few weeks ago at this party or that concert at Symphony. Grandy usually mumbles and takes another bite and Granny goes on talking about her golf game or her lunch at the club or how Hotsie is getting fat. When he hears his name, Hotsie comes over and barks, and Echo barks from the other room because there is a fence between the dogs to keep them from fighting for attention like they usually do when Granny and Grandy are home.

Tonight the sound of my chewing is louder because Granny and Grandy are unusually quiet. This makes me feel like I don't want to eat not only because the food is all leftovers from last summer on the boat but because the quiet means they are upset at each other and nobody likes to eat when other people are upset at each other. It hurts my tummy to do that. Grandy munches on his scrapple and stares at Granny with a look that makes it seem like he doesn't have a life inside him. Granny fidgets and lifts an empty fork to her mouth every once in a while and pretends it really has food on it and pretend-chews and pretends that everything is normal. They are upset at each other and that is why neither of them asks me any questions. I'm like the pretend food on Granny's fork because nobody can see me, either.

When Granny and Grandy are upset with each other it makes me think that anyone can go through their bad moods but when two people go through bad moods at the same time it makes it worse. But Granny and Grandy getting upset doesn't make sense to me because they are nice people and wonderful grandparents with grandkids who adore them to pieces and they ski and sail and have homes in Maine and in Nonquitt and they live in a small house on a big hill with shiny and delicate things inside. I let it go because I have learned that it's not worth it to keep thinking about these things because people don't make as much sense as the colorful and bright animals in cartoons that dance instead of just move.

Mom also cooks leftovers but they are not from last summer on a boat in Maine. Mom's leftovers are from her own cooking and they are usually from one or two nights before. The way Mom makes food is interesting because she's quick and neat. She never makes a mess and her food always turns out delicious. She doesn't make restaurant food, so it isn't fancy with different-tasting spices. It's usually spaghetti or lasagna or fish casserole or pot pie. Food like that. It is always warm and delicious and we never tell her this but I think she knows that's how we feel about Mom's cooking. The thing about Mom is that she doesn't sit with us while we eat. She starts cooking, she makes the dinner, and we eat it quickly because it's all boys except for me. Then she clears and usually does the dishes. I try to help her sometimes but she knows the procedure better than anyone so I have learned to stay away when she asks me to. Every so often she will ask one of my brothers to help her, but that's usually when she snaps in frustration that all she does is prepare food that we wolf down without even tasting it and then we get up from the table and leave a mess for her to clean up and it's just not fair. So one of my brothers will help her but she will still do most of the work and nothing feels any better. So we all go into our bedrooms and they do homework and I do my lists.

One night, Mom tries something different. She makes us liver and onions for dinner because it's what she and Dad grew up having once a week. We all come into the kitchen from the den where we were watching the news with Dad. As soon as I enter the kitchen I know it's not going to be a successful family dinner because the smell hits me like a wave of stench from the rabbit hutch when it hasn't been cleaned out in a month. The twins sense this, too, because I see Danny elbowing Kenny and Kenny whispering, "Stop." They both slow down as they approach the table, like they are trying to figure out an excuse for why they actually shouldn't be sitting down at that moment even though the clock says exactly seven o'clock and there is nowhere else in the world they should be except at the kitchen table eating dinner like the rest of the world is doing.

Robbie stomps heavy-footed down the stairs, enters the kitchen, and looks immediately crestfallen, as if he suddenly has a twenty-five-page paper to write and can't take time to eat with all of us. But he doesn't have a twenty-five-page paper to write because he is only in eighth grade and the longest paper he has ever had to write was five pages and I know this because the printer broke at five o'clock in the morning and he got so upset we all woke up while he threw a major temper tantrum and Dad had to drive to PIP Printing in order to get his five-page paper professionally printed. Robbie was embarrassed afterwards but he got an A minus, which made Dad say it was almost worth the meltdown but there is still a lesson in this, isn't there?

So we sit down to pretend enjoy liver and onions in order to make Mom happy. That's all we want to do. We don't need to ask each other about this. It is understood. There will be no rocking the boat. Without using words, my brothers and I decide we will all do our best to pretend-enjoy the liver and the reason we eat in small bites is because we want to appreciate every single bite. We want Mom to feel happy because of all the work she does for us in the kitchen and all the time like at five in the morning at Babson hockey rink in the freezing cold. The tension around the table thickens each time Dad says, "Wow, honey, you really worked hard on this!" or Robbie says, "Where did you get the recipe?" or Kenny says, "What part of the cow does this come from?" or Danny says, "I just love you so much, Mom!" At some point there is the moment where we actually must eat the carefully cut bite on our forks, and we do so together, like we are the group of high school kids holding hands and jumping off the bridge together on the Herring River at the Cape.

Instantly, we take our bite, chew, struggle, tear up in disgust, swallow with force, and look around at each other secretly even though nothing gets by Mom, who watches us like she has five eyes on her face, one glued to each of us, her brain assessing exactly what we think about her liver.

We hate it. We can't even try to hide the fact that we would eat anything – anything – rather than the plate in front of us. We would eat Brussels sprouts. We would eat mushrooms. We would eat rusty canned leftovers from Granny and Grandy's boat in Maine. We would gratefully eat anything besides the bitter, overwhelmingly gag-inducing gray meat on the plates in front of us. The game now becomes a question of who will dare speak first.

Danny is the baby turtle who pokes his head from the hole in the sand under swarming seagulls. I look at him as if he is taking it for the team and doing the most heroic thing he's ever done. With his characteristic toothy grin, he exclaims, "Mom, this is awful!" This moment perplexes me like no other. He insulted her cooking with a smile. He is killing her with kindness, as Dad would say.

The avalanche begins. "I can't eat this!" The plates are pushed away from our bodies. Even Dad says, "Perhaps this was the right idea but the wrong timing." At that, Mom explodes. "It's liver! This was our family tradition growing up and we turned out just fine! I worked hard preparing this for you—" That's when Robbie makes the fatal mistake of interrupting her with an empty compliment. He says, "I know that you worked hard, and we all appreciate it—" Then the final ultimatum from Mom, "Well, you can show your appreciation by eating every bite. You are not allowed to leave the table until you have eaten every bite from your plate."

As if trying to make lemons from lemonade, Dad tells us a story about Grandpops who stayed awake all night staring at the lima beans on his plate rather than eating them and going to bed. Dad told this story with a joyful spirit that unfortunately did not go well with the mood of the moment. In fact, it seemed to make Mom even more upset, because she asked him why he was trying to make fun of the hard work she put into making this perfectly delicious dinner.

The bubble pops a few minutes later when Robbie pulls the final straw. He places his silverware on his plate the way Mom and Dad taught him to when he is done with a meal. Like in France, they said, you place your fork and knife together on the plate facing at one o'clock. The knife-edge faces the fork. So Robbie does this. Danny quickly follows, as does Kenny. Mom's face gets redder and it is when I do the same thing with my fork and knife that Mom makes her final statement. She grabs Robbie's plate and, using his silverware, slides his liver and onions into Sandy's dog dish. "If you won't eat this food I worked so hard to make for you, at least the dog will!" Of course, Sandy runs to his dog dish and inhales the liver and onion. He looks up at Mom, swallows three times, and, with eyes that become droopy and crossed, throws up on the kitchen floor. My brothers all stare with eyes wide, covering their mouths. Dad also looks down but has the better judgment not to react. Robbie and my brothers can't help it and they suddenly burst out laughing. Loudly.

Mom says nothing. She turns around, removes her apron, tosses it down the basement stairs, and walks upstairs. We don't see her for the rest of the night. After cleaning up, we eat Cheerios for dinner and each go to our separate rooms for the rest of the night. It's the last night we have liver and onions at our house, and we never mention it again, out of respect for Mom who was only trying to share a meal she grew up eating when she was growing up with Granny and Grandy at their house in Weston where they didn't need to cook or drive or wash laundry for themselves because they had people to do all of those things for them so they could enjoy life.

Do They Know It's Christmas?

I have no idea what Dubonnet is. I just know I don't like it. Not one bit. Ever since I was little, Robbie and the twins have played a joke on me that they think is the funniest thing ever but I'm getting older now and I'm getting kind of tired of it. They will open the liquor cabinet and say, "Claire, here's your Dubonnet!" and they will pretend to open it and get ready to pour it and I will have to say no, thank you, and they will only stop after I say that. I used to think it was funny because the idea of drinking alcohol was something so silly for a young child. But now I'm a teenager and I really don't like being pretend-offered Dubonnet or rum or beer, even if it's meant as a joke. I don't like the taste of alcohol, and as I've gotten older I also don't like how it makes other people act when they drink it.

It's Christmas and my parents are having a party at our house. The liquor cabinet in the kitchen has been open for some time now, because many of my parents' friends and relatives enjoy cocktails. They leave the liquor bottles and the red leather ice bucket and the glasses and the sodas out on the counter next to the refrigerator, and the guests know that if they want cocktails they can go into the kitchen to get them. At Granny and Grandy's house, the liquor is in a room to itself. Here, it is in the kitchen, next to the door into the den. In order to get a good stiff drink, people need to find their way into the bright, yellow-painted and plastic-floored kitchen. Not exactly a place to rest and unwind with a rum tonic. So after filling their drinks, the guests head back into the living room or the den or the piano room to mingle and clink and laugh.

Robbie and the twins are the coat collectors and the hors d'oeuvres servers. They all look sharp in their jackets and ties, with their hair combed and parted and their best smiles. I look at Robbie, who is now much taller than the twins. He is preparing to sit at the piano and as he starts the first chords of 'O Come All Ye Faithful', I get a feeling in my tummy that is like I need to remember this moment right now because it is only right now that is important to remember. He plays Christmas songs with an incredible sense of meaning, like all of his heart has funneled into his fingers and through touch has been felt by the piano. The piano doesn't have feelings, but in this memory I see that it is no different than the bear and rabbit and deer that all talk to each other in the colorful cartoon. It's something I know that's not in my head but in my tummy and it is true. The music being played is music that everyone knows. But Robbie plays it from his heart through his fingers and the piano responds like it has a heart itself.

Then a moment happens that I couldn't forget even if I tried as hard as I could. Robbie asks the group whether he could play something that's not a Christmas carol, something that he's been working on for a while now. Everyone says yes and Robbie starts playing a piece I have heard before but I can't remember from where. It is a piano-only song, a song that wouldn't sound right if it was on a violin or even a flute. He plays it and Robbie is swaying with the music he is playing and the audience is silenced by the power of his love. He plays this piece, and I look over to Dad, who holds his eggnog with brown flakes on it. He is holding his eggnog with brown flakes on it and he sways with the rhythm just like his son. He sways with the rhythm like his son and he allows a tear to fall into the brown flakes on his yellow eggnog and he allows a tear to streak his cheek and he allows the streak to stay there for as long as it takes to become invisible because it has been removed from his cheek by the love of Robbie's piano playing that has taken over the entire piano room.

I'm happy to be in the piano room with my parents' friends and relatives. I'm happy to be there and not in the kitchen, where they make their cocktails. After Robbie finishes playing to thunderous applause, I make my way to the living room where I see our stockings all strung over the fireplace. There is a plate for Santa Claus, which has carrots and cookies already on it. I worry that Sandy will think they are for him, so I take the plate and move it to the table next to the fireplace. I will leave it there just until everyone leaves and we have gone to church and we return to home to get a good night's sleep on the night before Christmas.

One of my cousins is named Kip. I don't know him well because he is a distant cousin from California. As I lift the plate, Kip asks me what I'm doing. I say I'm moving the plate because it's going to get eaten by our dog, Sandy. I then ask him if he has a dog. Then he answers in a strange way when he doesn't answer me and just stares at my face. I wipe my nose and ask him again if he has a dog. Still, he doesn't answer. So now I need an answer to my question because I always need an answer before I let the question go. So I ask him again and he gets suddenly so mad

I feel my heart jump in my chest and I look around for a brother or close cousin. "Why do you ask the same question over and over again? Are you *retarded*?" I don't know how to answer because I haven't ever been told I'm retarded or not so I ask him if he has a dog. This seems to make him more upset and he asks me again if I'm retarded and he says that if I can repeat my question, well, then two can play that game. I ask again whether he has a dog because I need the answer to my question and I don't know the answer to his question and I hope that my question changes the subject but it doesn't. He asks me again if I'm retarded and at that point I begin to feel afraid all over again. All I want to do is go upstairs and sit on my bed with my pad and my markers and make my alphabet lists and feel the comfort of my routine.

A moment later, my close older cousin Richard comes over and puts his arm around my shoulder and he asks me whether he can get me a Dubonnet. My distant cousin Kip looks at him like he is eating breakfast for dinner. I look at Richard and instead of being frustrated by the same joke over so many years I answer him yes and I tell him I know exactly where it is kept and Richard and I walk away into the kitchen where he pulls me close to him and he says, "Claire, you never have to talk to that awful cousin again. He is from far away and he doesn't know how to be loving and kind like you are." Richard pours me a Sprite with ice and he squeezes lime into it and he hands it to me and he tells me he knows it's my favorite cocktail and didn't that Dubonnet joke work perfectly a moment ago.

I nod yes and when he offers his Coke glass for me to clink with my Sprite glass I do. But Richard stops me just as we are about to clink and he tells me to do it again but this time look him in the eyes because you can see the light of the soul through a person's eyes and he wants to see the light of my soul. I still look at the plastic kitchen floor for some reason. I want to lift my head and look at Richard's eyes, but I don't feel much light in my own. Richard guesses that and he says to me he thinks I'm not feeling much light and I nod.

He takes his fingers and gently lifts my chin and I look at his face and I see Dad's tear streaks on Richard's cheeks. I see Richard crying tears and it makes me want to cry tears of my own. But I can't show that I'm crying so instead I study Richard's tears and I try to understand his words when he says, "I'm crying because of how much I love you, Claire. I'm crying because of how much the world loves you. I'm crying because of how cruel the world can be to people like you. Beautiful. Pure. Clean. Full of peace. I'm crying for you but I'm not crying because I pity you. No, Claire. I wish I could be as kind as you." With that, Richard raises his glass again and I find my eyes looking into his and I don't look away. Instead, I find myself drawn to the flickering of white light in his black pupils. His chestnut-brown eyes are flickering in the middle and I see that his soul is light and warm and loving and that the world will have to push back very hard against the force of my cousin Richard's light.

We arrive at the Village Church at 10:45, which gives us enough time to find a pew with room for six people. There is a buzz in the air as people enter, looking put together, smelling like perfume and alcohol breath. I notice all the women reapplying lipstick right after sitting down. Then the head-turning begins. Robbie always cowers when Mom gets settled in the pew because she then starts looking all around the congregation to see who she knows. Her head becomes like the head of a swallow at the birdfeeder on the garage that we see through the kitchen window that the twins broke one time playing street hockey. She looks around in rapid movements, locking eyes with people she knows and waving hi. It's when she actually says, "Hi", that Robbie gets embarrassed. Tonight, Mom is quiet. She is just as connective because she's the church secretary and everyone knows her. But she's also I think remembering that it is Christmas Eve and it is the midnight service and it's not just the candlelight part that makes tonight an important time to be on our best manners.

I get more uncomfortable the longer we sit before the service begins because people keep stopping by the edge of our pew to say hi to us, especially to me. This isn't showing off, it is true. Ladies with hair sprayed like helmets and powerful perfume and the mint-alcohol combination from their breath. Many wear gold or silver pins on their dark red or green sweaters. They are happy to see me and for a moment I'm happy to see them. But I just want to settle in. I'm not in the mood to speak to people I only see in church. I feel particularly heavy tonight, and the conversation with my close cousin Richard remains in my head. This isn't an easy thing to let go of and I hope that as the service takes place I will be able to ease that episode from my memory books.

This is wishful thinking because this year I hear Mr. Gallagher talk about the light of the stars, of Mary's face, of the world when Jesus is born. Instead of listening to him, I think about what Richard said earlier tonight about the light in my eyes and its connection to my soul. I see the light all around the congregation, and I can clearly see the light from Mr. Gallagher's eyes as it shines from his pupils through our pupils. He speaks from the pulpit, and he speaks about the need for light during this dark time of the year. He speaks about the need for love and light and levity, which means being easy on each other and taking time to laugh. Mr. Gallagher's message is about those things, and I'm reminded of Richard and I think about how much he and Mr. Gallagher have in common and I wonder if Richard might ever want to be a minister because he might be very good at being one.

I'm awakened from these thoughts by the lights flickering off one by one. Without thinking, I reach for my white candle and hold it. Moments later, we pass the light from candle to candle and I say no thank you by shaking my head and Dad remembers that I choose not to hold fire in my hands because it is too dangerous if something slips. After all of the candles are lit, the violin begins playing 'What Child is This?' and we stand up as a congregation, as a village, as a collection of light-minded souls. Not long into the first verse, I feel the lump in my throat get bigger. I swallow over and over again, hoping to make it go away. But I know what is going to happen and I have learned not to fight it because these feelings are too strong.

I allow the lump to grow and I allow my eyes to get blurry with tears forming. Why is it always this song, I wonder to myself? I sing as best I can from memory because even if I could read from the hymnal I would not be able to read through my blurry tears. So I sing from memory and I feel the lump in my throat and I look around at the flickering soft golden light that has taken over the church and makes people's faces look like angels. Down the row of our pew, I see the serene and love-filled faces of all the members of my family. I catch Mom looking over at me and elbowing Robbie to do the same and Robbie visibly refusing to. He has seen me before during the candlelight part of the service and he does not need Mom reminding him that I cry every Christmas at the candlelight part of the service. I'm not an animal in the zoo. Nobody in the family means to treat me that way, but it does feel like it at this service, and I wish it would change, even if Christmas Eve takes place only once a year.

The family rule on Christmas is that nobody opens presents until everyone is in the living room. Once again this year I get yelled at by my brothers, who have "waited forever" for me to wake up. This Christmas, I agree with them because my clock says a few minutes after eleven. This is late. They are right. I don't know why but I have been sleeping later on weekends. During school, I have been tired and it is challenging for me to stay up to my nine o'clock bedtime. Anyway, today my brothers rip through their presents and they thank everyone, including Santa, who I continue to pretend-believe in because I think the twins still believe that he exists. I want to think this.

My gifts used to be surprises to me. I would receive coloring books, dolls, stuffed animals, puzzles, board games and clothes. This Christmas – and kind of last Christmas – my gifts have all been clothes. But not the main clothes I wear like tops and bottoms. It's the not-fun clothes like gloves, underwear, socks and hats that I'm opening. I'm glad to have these clothes, but now I have a lot of socks and underwear and I don't think I need so many hats and gloves, no matter how cold it gets outside.

My tummy says that Christmas is changing. Whether it is when Robbie was playing the piano or when I was standing in the kitchen with close cousin Richard or singing at church during the candle-lighting part of the service or right now sitting on the sofa surrounded by crinkled wrapping paper that no longer contains surprises inside but not-fun clothes instead, reminding me that the important things like not-fun clothes are becoming more important than toys and puzzles and coloring books and surprises that used to make me feel like people knew me better than I knew myself.

Take on Me

On Superbowl Sunday, we go to the Hudsons' house to eat chips, drink soda and order pizza from Domino's. I love going to the Hudsons' house. They have four kids like we do, and Dwight is one of my best friends. The parents are Judy and Carl, and they are very good friends with my parents. Judy and Carl always make me feel good because they always have fun ideas for when we are all together and we can choose to do them or not to do them. It doesn't matter to them. Judy is full of energy. She drives their four kids around everywhere. She is upbeat and always happy and she speaks with a voice that makes you want to listen to her. Carl is just plain funny. He is always joking around even though he is also very smart. He is often working outside when I visit, even in the freezing cold. Carl and Dad always take their sons pond skating and they also go to Bruins games together. Carl cut off two of his fingers with the log-splitter once, but even that didn't make him lose his laugh. I'm used to shaking his hand with the nubs where his fingers were. I don't think anybody even notices his missing fingers. I'm only reminded when I shake his hands or when he is outside still using the log-splitter. Dad says he got back on the bike. I've never seen him on a bike, but I've seen him on tractors, skis, sleds, ice skates, trucks, vans, and even stilts when one Halloween he was Uncle Sam. Carl and Dad drink wine together, and when Carl holds a glass of wine in the air in order to look carefully at it, he becomes suddenly very relaxed and he speaks like he is thirty years older than he is.

With four kids, their house is messy sometimes. They don't seem to care that much, because it seems like every time I go over there it isn't spick and span. At first, I feel like I want to clean it up for them because I like things organized and put in their place. After a while, I forget about the mess and I just end up having fun with Dwight.

Dwight is my age and he is a huge Patriots fan. Today, Dwight is wearing a puffy jacket that is red and blue and has the New England Patriots printed on the back. He has red and blue stripes smeared on his face. When I arrive, Dwight is talking with his father about numbers and points and what his father calls statistics. I'm impressed that Dwight knows so much about the Patriots and about football in general. I know that if I'm caught in a pinch, I can ask Dwight.

While hanging up my jacket I feel a cold smear on my face. I look over to find Dwight's younger sister Suzie gazing up at me with her face already painted. I hate getting things on my face. I hate make-up. I hate wearing barrettes in my hair and I hate how I'm feeling with paint on my face. Dwight wears a mask on his face when he sleeps at night and I don't know how he does it but I know he has to in order to breathe better and snore not so loudly. I want to push Suzie away, but she's little and young and it would not be a nice thing to do. Instead, I politely ask her not to do that any more and she promises she won't. Then I politely ask her if the bathroom is being used. It isn't, so I head in to the sink and wash off my face. I hope Suzie isn't upset that I told her no about the paint on my face. But she should know not to just come up to someone and surprise them by painting their face.

I'm in the kitchen with Judy and Mom when Jed arrives. I can tell he is here before I even hear him or see him. There is something that immediately changes in the room when Jed enters it, and it's not just me who thinks that. Kate and Cathy both agree that Jed is a special kind of boyfriend because he has a style that most guys don't have. I have to agree with them that he is kind of unique. If he wasn't, I would not have noticed him at the Special Olympics last summer in his purple shorts and green shirt. Since then, Jed and I have been trying to spend as much time together as we can. This takes work because he lives all the way in Abingdon, which is about an hour away. Jed has a younger sister who takes a lot of his time and he does martial arts. So he is busy. But we have gone to a movie, watched the circus when it was in Boston, and watched a Red Sox game from the bleachers. Granny hasn't offered her season ticket seats yet but I hope someday she does. Jed would be in seventh heaven.

All of these things are great, but the best times I have with Jed are when we are just sitting somewhere like in the back of the car or on a bench waiting for our parents or at a table waiting for the pizza to arrive. During those times we are usually not talking much with words but we are talking nonetheless and it is peaceful and warm and nice.

Today isn't going to be one of those special quiet times. Watching football brings out different things in people. It makes my twin brothers want to wrestle each other. It makes Robbie bored. It makes Dwight excited. It makes Carl and Dad louder with every beer they drink. It makes Mom and Judy talk in the kitchen, sitting with their elbows on the table and nodding in agreement with each other as if there are no disagreements in the world. I'm not sure about Jed and how he acts when there is football on the television. He warned me that he loves the Patriots and I told him about Dwight being the biggest Patriots fan I know so they should both get along just great. But this is the Superbowl. This is the biggest football game of the year and the Patriots are in it, so if a regular football game brings out different things in people, I can't imagine what the Patriots in the Superbowl might do. I will soon find out. In the meantime, I want to spend as much time with Jed as I can before he gets absorbed by the game.

Jed walks into the living room with his typical saunter. I call him over to the kitchen and he enters the doorway, stopping me in my tracks because he looks so handsome. He is wearing his track pants and Patriots sweatshirt. Underneath his Patriots sweatshirt is a button-down collared shirt and he is wearing sneakers with the laces neatly tied. He walks over to me with flowers in his hand and he gives me a hug. He tells me that the flowers are not for me – he has something else for me – they are for Mrs. Hudson. Judy responds with a gasp and a smile and a "You shouldn't have," and an "I know the perfect vase." Jed's cheeks get red and he contains a smile while stealing a glance at me, who can't keep my eyes off him. What a gentleman! What a clean-cut and handsome boyfriend I have! I want to give Jed a huge hug that lasts for a long time but I know that the time isn't right so I wipe my hands on my pants and offer him some chips and dip.

By the time the game begins, Jed has made friends with

everyone in the room. I'm pretty sure I overheard Dad saying to Carl he wishes he could offer Jed a beer. He's a year older than me, so he is sixteen, and he doesn't drink beer. I think he needs to obey the rules and I also don't think he will take well to beer. Something tells me this, and I don't know why. When Jed met Dwight, he took a few minutes to get used to how Dwight talks because of his Down syndrome. Jed patiently asks Dwight to please repeat himself so he can learn how he talks and Dwight does. Within a few minutes, they are talking all about the Patriots and they are trying to one-up each other about numbers and statistics. I have no idea what they are talking about but I do know that watching Jed get along so well with Dwight makes me feel like things are right in the world.

Suzie sits next to me still with paint on her face and she asks Jed whether he would like some paint on his face. I'm proud of Suzie for asking Jed because it shows that she learned from when she didn't ask me. Jed doesn't flinch before saying of course he would like his face painted. Suzie grins a mile wide and starts in on Jed's face. The Patriots could lose by a million points and I would still be having one of the best afternoons of my life.

And they do lose. Not by a million but apparently by enough points that the fans start leaving the game early and the commentators start speaking in lower voices without enthusiasm. Dwight holds out hope until the bitter end and so does Jed even though I can tell he is frustrated. No matter how many times he prayed for the guy with the headband to get injured, nothing seems to have helped the Patriots. The Bears celebrate with champagne sprays and hugs and joyful yelling and dancing to the Superbowl Shuffle. I don't remember much about the game except that the

Patriots lost by many points – and Jed earned many points with my friends and family…and especially with me.

As we leave, I see Dwight and Carl playing catch in the driveway, away from the cars. Dwight is running plays with the biggest grin on his face, as if the game never happened. He still wears his face paint, even though everyone else has washed theirs off. Carl throws the football in beautiful spirals and Dwight catches every single one, running and sprinting and jumping like one of the salmon in the waterfalls in Alaska. At one moment, he catches the ball and lands in a snowdrift as high as his waist. When I think about that catch, which was seemingly impossible, I remember it in slow motion, like the exceptional plays we saw on the television. And when I remember Dwight catching the ball in slow motion into a snowdrift as high as his waist and laughing with open eyes and deep guffaws of glee I feel proud of him.

Love is a Battlefield

I sit in the back seat of the car while Dad drives and Robbie sits in the other seat next to him. The Bruins trophy dangles from the sunroof opener and I wonder how many years we have had this car. Long enough for me not to remember the car Dad had before this one. I look behind me to the dried-up bees in the crease at the bottom of the rear window that are impossible to remove. There are cars behind us because it is a busy Friday afternoon and we are on our way to the Cape for Memorial Day weekend. Robbie sits facing forward and is talking with his hands as Dad has his hands placed on the wheel and his sunglasses on. The trees are becoming more dried-out-looking, and the landscape is becoming flat and the sides of the road are beginning to show sand on the edges so I know we must be approaching the bridge. The name of the game is whoever sees the Golden Arches first gets a large size of whatever he wants. I'm not that hungry, but I like to play this game, so my eyes are peeled.

They are talking about the new school Robbie will go to next year for high school. Robbie is talking about how much he would like to go to the local high school but going to the private school farther away is fine, too, as long as he can go to confirmation class and see his town friends as much as he can.

Dad is encouraging him, telling him that the private school will help him to study better, not harder. They spend an awful lot of time talking about what better not harder means and I start to tune them out, peering ahead to find the Golden Arches before they do. I'm looking for the prize but thinking about Jed while the trees rush by in a blur. It has been a long time since I met him at the Special Olympics and he tells me he is in love with me. I don't know whether I feel the same way but it doesn't matter because it's just words and my feelings are happy when I see him and when I think about him. Kate calls him a diamond in the rough. Dwight still likes him from when they met at the Superbowl party. Cathy squeals about how cute he is and Jeannie doesn't like to talk about these things like boyfriends.

Thinking about Jed makes me feel a little bit like I must be growing up because girlfriends and boyfriends happen when people are teenagers and like on television when Marcia gets together with George the football player they are older and grown-up. When Nancy dates the guy her dad doesn't approve of and dates him anyway, she's trying to be grown-up, too. I see Robbie growing up and soon he will have a girlfriend and that will be quite a new turn of events. But for me, I have a boyfriend and I feel not that grown-up because I don't drive a car or wear my boyfriend's letter jacket. We get together on weekends and our parents or his older sister drive us places and that doesn't make us feel very grown-up, either. But when we are actually watching the movie together in the dark theatre, and when I feel his knee touch mine or his greasy hand in the popcorn bucket, every bit of my feelings tell me that I'm old enough to feel this way and I want more of it while I also don't know what lies ahead. All of this is in my mind while Dad and Robbie talk about getting older and going to a new school and learning how to study better, not harder.

I stop thinking about Jed because Dad just said something to Robbie that made no sense. Robbie just told Dad that he thinks the world of him. He said that he will always look at him like a hero and someone he wants to be like because of his values and his advice that is always right to follow. Dad said that will not always be the case and that there will be times up ahead where he will not respect him and he will be angry with him. Robbie said he can't imagine that ever being the case, not in a million years, and Dad said just wait.

Just wait.

What am I waiting for? What will my future be like? Will Jed be in it? Will Dad? Will I be picked up by Mike the van driver every morning in the future? Will I be going to school until I'm old? Will I be living at home for years and years and years? If Dad believes that the future will be so different with Robbie that he tells him to just wait, does this mean that my future can also be completely different? Am I going to just wait to see how much my life will change? How long will I have to wait? What will be the result of waiting? How many pads of paper with lists and letters will I fill up before I get the answer?

"I see the Golden Arches!" Robbie beat me. He got the McDonald's sign before I did and I wasn't even in a conversation with Dad like he was. I should have kept my eyes on the prize. I should have just told myself to wait and not allow my questions to take over my brain. Fortunately, they have started to go away because they are not the kind of questions that make sense to keep in my brain because they don't have answers that can be spoken. Sometimes the only answers to questions are told through experiences and not words. Sometimes the only question that should take over the mind is, "Where are the Golden Arches?", and the answers to all the other questions swarming around will fall into place when they are good and ready. Sometimes the best advice is to "just wait" and you'll get the extra fries anyway because your brother is good at sharing and he knows that I was trying to win this game even without me telling him.

Part of growing up means getting moody about things that didn't bother you when you were younger but bother you a lot now that you're going through changes. I find myself getting moody about the order of my stuffed animals or the pictures tacked on the bulletin board above my dresser. I find myself getting moody about Sandy's dog-breath or the way Mom has to weigh everything she eats on a scale before eating it. Sometimes she makes me do the same thing, and it makes me very moody because I'm skinny as a rail like Granny says. I get moody when I sleep late on weekends but I also get moody over my brothers playing street hockey outside or the sound of Robbie thumping down the stairs to get breakfast before heading out to soccer. I get moody when Robbie plays the piano wrong or when dinner is late. I get moody when the music in the van is too much guitar or when Kate has a tuna fish sandwich for lunch and it smells up her entire lunchbox. I get moody when Jed doesn't call me at seven thirty like he says he will and when he calls but doesn't really want to talk so all I hear is breathing on the other side of the line and I have no idea why he is so keen on wasting his time and mine.

Part of getting moody is also about dealing with it. On the phone with Jed, I tell him how I feel. After seven minutes of just listening to him breathing on the other end of the line, I tell him that I've got to go. That really puts a crank in his day because he starts speaking again with questions like why do I need to go and why do I get bored on the phone with him and why don't I love him like he loves me? His voice rises and gets louder and he continues asking questions like who is the new guy and why won't I be faithful and when are we going to get engaged? My palms sweat and I feel the flutters in my heart turn into thuds. My brain freezes up and all I can tell him is I got to go. But I don't go. I stay on the line and just listen as Jed gets more and more angry. Robbie is doing homework at the dining room table and he makes eye contact with me and I ignore it because he knows what is going on and that is fine. Jed's questions begin to get meaner as he gets more angry. He asks why I don't kiss him like he wants me to and why do I hang out with Cathy so much and why can't I spend more time with him but not in my sweatpants? I tell him I've got to go and he continues throwing questions my way that he doesn't want the answer to but questions that make him feel better just by asking them even if they make me feel worse. By the time I realize Jed is going through a major temper tantrum my "I gotta go, Jed" is met with a splashy sound and then nothing. Silence. Pause for thought, I think to myself. Oh no, wait a sec.

He was speaking to me from the bathroom. Sometimes it's the only place he can find privacy. When I think about it, his voice was echoing and he was running the faucet every so often to splash water on his face because he tells me that's the best thing to do when he gets hot under the collar. Jed was talking to me and asking me all those questions while having his crank turned from the bathroom. The noise and the tension and the echoing all blended into one fact. I turn to Robbie, who is already looking at me with a questioning expression like, what's going on?

I think he flushed his phone down the toilet.

After hanging up the phone like Robbie told me to, I sit in the dining room chair feeling like I need to just take a break from all of it. I need to step away from his moodiness that can be anger. He already once broke some light bulbs around the mirror when he was upset at me for something that happened a long time ago. But flushing his phone down the toilet is a new level of bad behavior that I need to pay attention to. Maybe it's like what Dad told Robbie in the car back in the summer, that sometimes you're not going to like the person you love for reasons outside of your control. My reasons for not liking Jed are pretty clear after this phone call. Robbie agrees. He suggests that Jed and I take a break for a while. Just wait. Jed can learn how to manage his anger better because Robbie even noticed that the way Jed has been with me lately isn't exactly tender and loving behavior. I agree but it is very hard to agree with him because it means that I believe that Jed has not been treating me very well lately and that my palms have been sweaty around him and that since Day One he has shown me that he gets temper tantrums. Maybe taking a break is the right idea. Just wait. I can take time for myself and then maybe get back together with him. By flushing his phone down the toilet, doesn't it seem like he was kind of breaking up with me? I'm sad but also relieved at that suggestion because I hate to be the bad guy especially when it's someone I love.

A lot of grown up relationships is about just wait. Just wait until the sadness is over. Just wait until I can feel fine again. Just wait until Granny makes tea and we laugh and talk about England and Juliet and right then at that moment we decide to go to

London together this summer because lifelong friends are like wine and not Dubonnet. Just wait until I have no more confusion about why I'm moody and tired all the time. Just wait until the pain goes away and then I can let go of his memory like I let go of questions that don't have clear answers no matter how many times I ask them. Just wait until I see Jed again and we decide to break up for real because we are both growing up and it is up to us to decide to grow up apart like mature grown-ups making grown-up decisions like I see on television and with my parents and with my brother Robbie when he talks with Dad about how much he loves him only to be told that love isn't going to be this way forever.

Sweet Dreams (Are Made of This)

Robbie does a paper route every morning before school. He sets his own alarm and wakes up at five thirty and he gets out of bed and puts on warm clothes and walks down the driveway and takes wire cutters and clips the wires holding the stack of newspapers together and he puts the stack of newspapers in his newspaper bag with a bright orange shoulder strap and he walks down the driveway into the road with a limp because the side the newspaper bag is on is heavy and makes him bend in that direction. I watch Robbie do this from my bedroom window. Every morning he does this. In the winter when it is dark outside he carries a flashlight with him and he walks down the driveway into the road with a limp and feet that can slip from underneath him because of the ice. These quiet mornings are when Robbie gets the newspapers to our neighbors. It is still and quiet and not even a car in the street when he walks down the driveway into the road with a limp. On Sundays he needs to slip the advertisements into the main newspaper and this takes time but it's also not important to explain. The bottom line is Robbie delivers the newspapers to our neighbors in order to make money so he can treat our family to something special like *Cats*. He has done this since he was in sixth grade. He tells me it feels good to be outside in the lonely darkness delivering newspapers to our neighbors. It makes him feel good. And it also makes him earn money. The twins are too young and I'm too special. So this leaves only Robbie to make money.

When Robbie made enough money to do this, he tells us that he will buy us tickets to see *Cats* together as a family. Actually, he tells us that he already bought the tickets to see *Cats* together a week ago. He heard a song from *Cats* on the radio and immediately called the theater and asked for six tickets to see *Cats* with his family. He was told that he needed a credit card, so he snuck into Mom's purse and used her credit card and he kept the cash from the newspaper route in an envelope that he gave to Mom when he told her that he bought tickets to see *Cats* together as a family. Now Robbie is telling us this news, and the twins are both excited, even though they haven't heard any songs on the radio and that is all right. Sometimes just the twins being excited is the important part. When Robbie tells us all that he bought tickets for us to see *Cats* together as a family, Mom's eyes get teary and she has a smile that is more peaceful than the Herring River at high tide. Dad isn't with us when Robbie tells us about how he used his paper route money. But he is sure to be the first person ready to go when the evening approaches. Dad is the first person down the stairs, wearing a jacket and tie and smelling like Old Spice. I'm excited about going to see *Cats* with my family, especially with Dad all dressed up like this and with Robbie making hard-earned money from his lonely paper route that he enjoys during the silence of early morning.

Cats does not disappoint. The show is about a bunch of cats that live in the same area of the city together. There are cats that are alone, cats that are in love, cats that are happy, cats that are jealous, cats that are angry and cats that are complicated. The songs are fun and they have pizazz with energy and spark. There are a lot of songs when cats sing together under a spotlight with the stage dark behind them. The show doesn't really tell a story but I think it has a lot to do with being a part of a group of cats that form like a family together. There are times when the cats support each other and also fight each other and also sing with each other like they've had too much to drink. *Cats* is high energy. Until the song called 'Memory' plays and suddenly we are mopping up our tears from the floor. When I hear this song and when my skin gets goose bumps and when I find my vision getting shimmery because it is just too purely beautiful and lonely a song, I look over at Robbie. I know this is the song that made him spend his hard-earned money from his lonely paper route that he enjoys during the silence of early morning. I also know the tears welling up in my eyes are for and because of my brother Robbie.

We bought Sandy after Coco died from being old. It was five years ago when Sandy came into our house as a puppy and we all fell madly in love with him. Sandy is named after the dog in the first musical I saw, called *Annie*. The one with the girl with the tight perm of orange hair that matches her dress she wears during almost the entire play. It makes you wonder when she gets it cleaned or does she have a closet full of the same orange dresses that match her tight perm of orange hair? The musical is fun and whiny and before you get tired of all the kids complaining about their lives we enter a huge mansion and the story really takes off and Annie comes out on top not

126

only because of her hair matching her orange dress but because she ends up being a very good person we can all respect. Annie's dog is named Sandy. Sandy is a yellow dog and the dog we got is a yellow dog so we decide to name him Sandy, too. I'm glad we did because I can't think of a better name for this dog who is so fun and so playful and who loves rolling around on the sandy beaches on the Cape.

When we get the word that Sandy needs to be put to sleep because he has cancer, the den becomes covered in the blanket of sadness that has only happened a few other times in our lives. Yet this time we are older. Robbie is in high school and the twins are growing like weeds at Dad's school. I'm still going to my school and my van driver is no longer Mike because Mike had to move to Rhode Island so now we have Danny who is a nice driver who plays the radio too loudly. It's all right, though, because my friends wear Walkman headphones. I don't like to wear them because they feel like barrettes on my head and it doesn't feel comfortable, like I'm wearing jewelry on my head or something like that. But I don't mind that my friends wear their headphones because it makes them happy when Danny plays the music too loud. I can hear their music through the headphones so I also feel like I'm a little bit a part of what they're listening to. It's all right.

Robbie is in high school and we are seeing him a lot less now than when he was at Dad's school like the twins still are. His school is also a place where students sleep so he sometimes sleeps at the school and I don't see him for days on end. I still have Wednesday nights with Granny and Grandy and that is good for the family because it gives Mom and Dad time alone with the twins so they don't get too distracted, especially when Robbie is staying overnight at his school. It is good. All of it. And Sandy is a big part of why it is good. He grew up with us and he was there for us whenever we needed to give a pat, toss a ball, or swim in the Herring River.

Now we are being told that Sandy will no longer be with us and that he will be joining Coco in Doggie Heaven. This immediately makes my heart clamp tight while the blanket of sadness lands on all of us in the den of silence. This is a horrible message to receive after a great dinner and a funny episode of *The Cosby Show*. Suddenly, Danny leaps off the sofa and in one full sweep lands softly on Sandy who is lying in the middle of the floor. He lands on Sandy and Kenny lands on top of him and even Robbie joins the dog pile. They just lie there, huddled together as brothers who love their dog so much it hurts. Danny looks up at me and signals me with his hand to come over and join their big hug. I shake my head no because I think there is enough hugging going on in front of me and I don't need to join in this action in order for Sandy to know how I feel about him leaving us soon.

At the right time, Dad asks the boys to get off the dog and they do and they sit back where they were before the group hug. He asks me and the boys to think back on our favorite times with Sandy and to say them out loud and to thank him for those memories. Dad asks Mom to join us all, and she at first says she's busy doing the dishes but in a few moments I see her in the doorway in her apron, leaning against the doorway with an expression telling me that this is a very important time right here, right now and that Sandy is bigger to us than just a pet. The boys thank Sandy for the time he ate the chocolate cake and spent the whole night running up and down the stairs because he had so much sugar in his system. They thank Sandy for when he ate the tomato plant and grew more tomato plants from his poop. They thank him for the balls he fetched in the Herring River, on the beach, in the backyard. They thank him for his dog-breath, for him throwing up in order to save us from eating Mom's liver and onions, for trying so hard to chase the Frisbee he tripped on his own leash.

There was a lot of laughter that night before Sandy went away from us forever. The memories were fun and funny, and they helped my brothers hide their sadness. This is true because it would have been much easier to thank Sandy for the times he was there for them. The time when Robbie talked to him after being caught playing with my dolls. The time when the twins were hiding from a group of older kids in the neighborhood and Sandy scared them all away. The times when Robbie, on his way out to clip the wire from the stack of papers in the earliest hours of the morning, had Sandy with him for company as he slugged the bright orange shoulder strap on his shoulder, leaned into the heavy weight of the newspaper bag, and shuffled through the snowy driveway and onto the street with his dog as his only company in the stillness of the snow-blanketed dawn.

Those are my memories of Sandy and they make up my memory of my family growing up as the world becomes a bit darker like the stage where the cats stood together and sang with energy and chaos and community and love. So when those moments of memory emerged and became clear, we all got goose bumps from the purity and peace at the core of each. Those memory moments illuminate even those of us who are most hidden in the darkness.

If This Is It

When things around me get dizzy and busy with people coming in and out of the doorways and voices rising and falling with different needs to be heard and all I see are purples, greens and oranges streaking this way and that, I take time out for myself. With Robbie in high school and the twins growing up and Mom and Dad starting a new job at their new printing store they work at together and no dog to pat and play with, I'm more by myself. Even when the noise is louder and the breeze from everyone moving by is always on my face. Sometimes I need this time to be by myself and sometimes I don't. I try not to get involved when everyone is busy so I will go upstairs to my room and do my own thing.

Ever since I was little, I have enjoyed making lists. I take out my blank pad of paper and a marker from my bin and I write my name over and over again. If I get tired of that, I will write another name like "Kate" over and over again. Sometimes it's not a name but just a letter I will write over and over again. I do this because it feels good. I remember once when my cousin Christina tried to help me by telling me where I'm getting my letters down wrong. It did not go down well because I became frustrated because I was only thinking about how wrong my writing was instead of how good the feeling of writing is for me. I did not make my list much longer with Christina that day and I changed the subject to something else like having an imaginary tea party, which was pretty forgettable.

I have a skin thing that the doctor says not to worry about so I don't. But it seems to bother Mom a lot because it looks like I have scabs all over my arms and legs sometimes. I know this sounds gross, and when I think about it, I guess it is. But it doesn't hurt me to have these scabs and like I said they come and go. When I feel like I need to be alone but I can't then I will itch a scab. Not that long, and not that hard. But sometimes the itching can make a scab look worse than it was before and there isn't anything I can do about it. This is what makes Mom upset, I think, because when I wear shorts and a short-sleeve shirt all you can see are the scabs if that's all you want to see. On my face I never get scabs because it doesn't feel the same to scratch your face as your arms and legs. Besides, Jed tells me I have a pretty face, so I don't want to mess it up. Still, the arms and legs are my doing and I agree that it would be good to stop doing the itching and find another way to relax and unwind and let Calgon take me away like the television commercial says.

When I think about it, there is another thing I do when I notice that the clocks are not telling the same time or the twins are in an argument or Robbie is being moody or Dad hasn't been home in a while and we are waiting and waiting for him in order to have dinner on our plates. I will rock back and forth in my chair. The funny thing about it is that I don't notice that I'm doing it. Someone else needs to point it out to me and once they do I try to stop but it's hard to do that once the ball has started rolling. By rocking I'm able to block out the things that irritate me and that I can't change myself, like the clocks. The rocking doesn't harm anyone but I suppose it can be distracting. I close my eyes when I do this, and I lose track of where I am, and that can be like waking up a sleepwalker because I get startled when someone yells at me to *stop.*

When I'm dancing, there is nobody there to tell me to stop. I'm watching the colorful lights spin around me and all the other people here tonight at the Spring Dance at the Parkland Rec Center from seven thirty until nine. The other people are all the same because all I see are black shadows with rainbow circles passing all over them like the colors on the wall when the sun shines through the stained glass window just right. I sometimes get scared in the dark, like when I'm at the Cape and walking the path from the Sumner house to ours after the sun has set. But at a dance, I only feel safe because everyone here is a friend of mine and we are surrounded by the music we love. We bump into each other but it's all right, it happens. We dance as a group sometimes and other times we dance with one person only. I'm dancing with Kate, Keith, Dwight and Christine when Jed approaches. I haven't seen Jed since he flushed the phone down the toilet and the butterflies come back to my tummy.

Jed makes his way directly to me and I think he wants to dance but as soon as he approaches I can see that he has other things in mind. He takes my arm and he walks me over into a darker corner that the colored circles seem to miss. I hate when someone grabs my arm and he knows this so this is why I know he is upset with me. He starts talking at me with a look in his eyes that tells me he isn't happy, even though 'I Saw the Sign' is playing and that song makes everyone happy. But not Jed tonight.

He is talking at me and I have no idea what he is saying because the music is loud. But I can tell by his eyes that he is upset and I think he is upset at me and I don't know what to say back to him except okay and yes whenever there is a pause in the conversation and his eyes look at me like they are waiting for a response. So I agree to whatever he says, and it seems to not help after all and instead it seems to make him more upset at me. I begin to get afraid because of his temper and because he is gripping my arm more tightly the longer we are in the corner together and he knows how much I hate having my arm gripped for a long time.

As the corner we are in together gets even darker and as Jed talks to me in words I can't understand yet eyes I understand only too well, my memory takes over and I think back to a world full of color and brightness. Jed and I are at the Special Olympics together and we are introducing ourselves with him in the purple shorts and green shirt that reminds me of the Bahamas. I'm wearing a medal that I won after Kate fell down and we re-did the race. I remember walking together on another sunny day and getting ice cream and telling him that I love peppermint stick but I don't like chocolate and him telling me that is ridiculous and that chocolate is the best flavor that has ever existed. My memories taking over are all like this. Sunny days and blue skies and conversations when we can disagree on things like ice cream and everything is still all right and the tingling feeling and the wide feeling in my heart takes over.

But now I need to snap back to reality and walk away from the handsome and beautiful young man who loves me I know. I need to move away from him and walk toward my future without him. I tell him all of this when I take my hand on his grip and remove it from my aching arm. His grip loosens immediately – he never understood the power of his anger – and he gives me a curious look as I slide away from him, walking backwards and looking at him with "goodbye" all over my face, flashing as brightly as possible like road construction signs so he can't possibly not see my message. Jed's shadow faces into the dark-on-dark corner of the gym as I feel another hand on my upper arm – this time a soft hand and a warm hand.

I turn to face the person whose hand is so softly placed on my upper arm and I see that it belongs to Kate, who has over time become my best friend except for Juliet. She also doesn't talk and instead stares into my eyes like saying everything is going to be all right. She allows me to tell her about my heart breaking and my sadness and my pain through my eyes and she allows me to take all the time I need. She by now has both her hands on my shoulders and she doesn't break our eye-to-eye connection until the time is right and that time happens when the entire 'Purple Rain' finishes, including the guitar at the end, that goes on for many minutes yet tonight feels like only seconds. When I rock back and forth over the weeks and months ahead, I hear 'Purple Rain' in my head over and over again and it is only the guitar part at the end and it feels better to rock and hear this music but it is never completely satisfying. Like itching my scabs. Like writing pages of lists. Like watching my twin brothers fight and there isn't anything I can do except stare at my clenched fist.

More Than Words

My twin brothers were always easy for me to tell apart. I could tell them apart before my parents could. This isn't because Kenny wears red and Danny wears blue. It's not because of their faces being different shapes. It's not because Kenny is just a little bit taller than Danny. It's not because Kenny holds his hockey stick with his right hand and Danny holds his in his left hand. Danny and Kenny are different people in the way they feel and the way they communicate. This is something I noticed only a little while ago. Before then, I could not really understand why telling them apart was such a snap. Danny's bright smile and Kenny's warm thoughtfulness are like two different glows. If I could give them colors based on their glows, Danny would be yellow and Kenny would be London bus red. I guess Kenny's color is perfect for him. Danny wouldn't look good wearing yellow sweaters, so I guess blue is good for him. The funny thing is that even though Robbie wears green, he should be wearing blue because it is his favorite color and it is definitely his glow. Open like the sky and soothing like water, but he could also get very cold, which has been happening more often lately because he has become moody while he has been growing up and maybe Dad on that car ride was right.

When I met Kate at the Special Olympics, I had trouble understanding her at first. Not because she was hurt or because she looked like she was from a different country. She speaks weakly and it is as if her throat needs to work extra hard to get the voice out. She told me once that her throat is broken and that she can't swallow hard and that is why she drools a lot. It is also why she takes pink liquid before she eats. It is also why she does not lie down during the day or for an hour after dinner. Kate can't eat steak or chicken from the grill unless it is put through the blender, which she thinks isn't very tasty. I don't blame her. So she chooses smoothies and soups and things like that.

Because of Kate's broken throat, she can't speak with clear words. Cathy says that her words blend together and that they are thick like molasses. She gets irritated by this, so Kate doesn't talk to her very often because she makes Kate feel stupid. I think Cathy is being selfish and that if she only put in more effort she would understand Kate clearly. It's not like I have a magic skill and can understand her like she speaks in code or something. They are English words and it just takes time to get into the flow of her talking. Once you're in that flow, it's like you're on a raft down the river and her voice is no longer molasses but more like Sprite instead. Bubbles and sweet and tangy and full of surprising words in the ingredients.

Kate has a wicked sense of humor and you only need to spend a few bits of time with her to realize it. Even if you don't understand her words, you understand her message and her message usually starts out by saying something funny about the person she's talking to. If someone very tall approaches her, Kate will say something like, "Well, aren't you a giant." If someone with a bad attitude approaches her at CVS where she works, she will say, "Turn that frown upside down!" Maybe it is good that Kate is hard to understand because if she wasn't I could see her getting into a lot of bad situations. One thing I know for sure is that Kate will never say something about someone who is sad or fat or with visible special needs. She will make funny comments about babies who cry or spit up. She will not make funny comments about Donna in her wheelchair.

Kate loves the Boston Red Sox as much as Dwight loves the Patriots. She has seven Red Sox hats, and two of them are green. Kate's head is usually covered by a Red Sox hat, which keeps the sun from burning her hair. She wears cheap plastic sunglasses and she has a lot of those, too. Rainbows, Red Sox, pink flamingoes, Mickey Mouse and more. She loves her cheap plastic sunglasses and she does not let them get in the way of her ability to show her smiling eyes. Kate dresses in bright colors, including the pink and yellow bowling jacket that has her name on the back of it. That is her favorite jacket. She wears white Velcro sneakers like I do, and she loves wearing plastic and colorful jewelry, like I don't.

One day, Kate is over at my house and we are upstairs in my bedroom and she looks at the pads of paper and markers on my desk and she says to me that I spend too much time upstairs in my room with my paper and markers. I say, *No I don't*, and then she lays into me like my lists and drawings are wasting my life away and that I need to go downstairs more and besides, why do I wear such dull and boring clothes? Her disappointment in me hurt me in my tummy but quickly she made a joke of it. She said that she knows I'm feeling upset at her for being so honest but it is because she cares about me so much and she wants me to spend more time with people. It is a good thing to do, she says, and it wouldn't hurt if I started wearing more colorful clothes like she does because it's a way to make people smile – even people you don't talk to but instead just watch you from the other side of the street. I've seen that happen when walking with Kate and it's like when you see a person walking a pretty dog like Sandy was. I miss how strangers would smile first at Sandy, then at me and whomever I'm with, then at themselves as their mind thinks about all the happy memories of dogs in their own life.

When I got back from a trip to visit Juliet last summer, Vicki asked me whether I learned how to take the piss out of someone when I was in England. I did not know what that meant. So she told me that it is the same thing as making people laugh by making fun of things about them. Kate is an expert in taking the piss out of people. She is particularly good at taking the piss out of my brothers. The first thing she ever said to Robbie when she met him was "I'm gonna *get* you!" Robbie asked her to repeat herself and she did and from then on Robbie and Kate had this joke about her getting him. Kenny and Danny are her crushes. She wishes they were older because if they were she would date them both at the same time, she says. I ask her why not Robbie and she says that he is too silly for her. If only she knew what he is like when nobody is watching, she might feel differently.

Kate has won the Best Worker Prize at CVS three times. She has each one framed in her bedroom at her house. She knows where everything is, so when a customer asks her for Aqua Fresh toothpaste, she instantly points them toward Aisle 9. Deodorant is Aisle 3 and so on. Everyone loves Kate at CVS because she's a hard worker when she's putting things in their proper place and she's also very helpful and fun and nice. I struggle sometimes watching her at CVS because I understand everything she says, and she says everything right, but the customer asking the question can't understand so she asks the same question again and again, usually louder each time. I want to interrupt and tell the customer, *It's Aisle 5*, but that might make Kate feel like she can't be understood even when she's trying her hardest and even though people like me can understand her every word.

One time there was a group from the middle school who came in and they were all in a bad mood because they went right to Kate and began asking her questions about where is everything. She answered as best she could, but she forgot some of their questions because they all came at her so fast and furious. But then they started imitating what they heard from her broken throat and weak voice and it was not the same as taking the piss out of her. The boss at CVS finally noticed that this was going on and he kicked out the boys after getting their names on the back side of a receipt. Kate continued putting away the Bic pens in Aisle 1 and she finished up her day. But she felt sick for five weeks afterwards, or at least that's what she said as an excuse for not going to work even though she was just fine in the van and at school and in the van going back home again.

Granny has a friend named Mrs. Hinman. Mrs. Hinman smokes brown cigarettes and lives in Connecticut with her dogs. She drinks her cocktail in an upside-down triangle glass that spills when she throws back her head and laughs with a voice that sounds like a trumpet. Granny and I watched a movie with her once and she laughed with that trumpet laugh and she had to be shushed by the people around her and Granny raised an attitude with the people after the movie was over. I can't remember how it settled out, but I also understand where they were coming from. Mrs. Hinman laughs so hard that it moves from being something that is contagious like yawning to something that makes you want to grab her by the arm and say stop. The trumpet laugh does not make you feel like laughing when you hear it because it does not sound quite right. It is like when Robbie plays a bad note in a piano piece. We all know it isn't quite right for the song. Mrs. Hinman's laugh has always sounded not quite right. Too loud and too trumpety and too much effort. I do chuckle on the inside when she spills drops from her cocktail because it is funny to watch adults spill drinks.

The thing about Kate is that she wears her bright colors and she laughs with water in her eyes because she truly finds many things wickedly funny to the point of crying. She doesn't push it like Mrs. Hinman does. She dresses like a rainbow because why not? She says hi to everyone at CVS because people are good in their hearts, even when they do bad things like those middle school boys. She told me that those boys just need to grow up and did I notice that one of them had his zipper down the whole time? His fly was down and how can you take someone seriously when his fly is down? She tells me this and breaks into laughter because it is true that you can't take someone seriously when his fly is down. Through my own laughter, I tell her that I agree and that *sometimes kids just need to grow up.*

Drive

We celebrate Robbie getting his driver's license with ice cream at Emack & Bolio's, which is only a mile away but Robbie insists on driving Dad's car with the Bruins trophy dangling from the sunroof handle. He insists on driving all of us to get our ice cream. Mom gives him a ten-dollar bill and tells him to drive safely and Robbie says he knows because it is precious cargo and Mom smiles to herself. Danny sprints for the front seat and Kenny and I open the back door and shuffle into the back seat. I reach for my seat belt and click in. Robbie reaches his arm behind Danny's head as he turns his neck to look behind him as the car moves in reverse down the driveway. Instantly he looks more grown up just by doing this and I feel like time is moving too fast. As he drives down our street, I see his blue eyes in the rear-view mirror and I think how much his eyes are starting to look like Dad's. It is like the song Vicki sings about the father and son. That song never used to mean much to me until now.

Getting our ice cream isn't anything special except for when the man behind the counter asks Robbie what I want and he turns to me and asks me what I want. I get mixed up when he does this because I'm not used to being asked what I want because Mom usually orders for me. "Claire would like

141

the burger with a side salad and a Sprite." When I'm asked about what ice cream I want, I look back at Robbie who tells me that this is my decision, not his. The man behind the counter shifts weight on his legs and sighs. I look at the line behind me and the many flavors of ice cream in the freezer. The man behind the counter taps his fingers on the freezer and Robbie stares him down while telling me to take my time, others can wait.

The air in the store becomes tight and I tell him I'll just have vanilla in order to be able to sit down with the twins, who are already shooting spitballs at each other with their straws. Robbie asks if that is what I really want because vanilla is kind of boring and it's not like they don't have peppermint stick or mint chocolate chip. Before I can change my mind the man behind the counter says that he guesses it's vanilla then and Robbie tells him to wait a sec and the man behind the counter sighs, this time loud enough that Robbie asks if there is a problem and the man lurches back with his hands raised and says no, there is no problem. But he says this while looking at the other people in line, especially at the woman who looks at her watch.

Vanilla is fine. I want vanilla. It's fine.

Sometimes it's better to just make a decision in order to make the decision. When it's ice cream it's not like you can go wrong. Ice cream is ice cream and it is always a treat no matter what the flavor. Unless it is rum raisin. As Dad would say, rum raisin is a no-brainer.

Driving one mile for ice cream is one thing. Driving into Fenway Park is another thing entirely. Dad talks about how being a Boston driver is a blessing and a curse because if you can drive the narrow streets and deal with the jerky drivers you deserve a medal. But being able to drive with all the jerky drivers means you need to be a bit jerky yourself so it is also a curse. In order to prove yourself as a Boston driver, you need to get into a fender bender, get a speeding ticket, get several parking tickets and master what he calls the Boston Swerve, which means going from the far left lane to the far right lane without using your signals and in one fell swoop. Mom hates when Dad talks like this. She reminds him that we are from the suburbs, not Boston and he shrugs, saying that it's a mindset, whatever that means.

So the twins and I are squeezed in the back seat of Dad's Volvo while Robbie and Granny sit in the front seat. Granny smells familiar, like Chanel No 5 and wool. Dad's old Volvo feels like a fancy car like Mr. Price's fancy car because Granny is in it. She is dressed in a silk blouse tucked into khakis and a black belt with gold buckles. The only thing different than usual about Granny is the Red Sox hat on her head. Otherwise, she looks just the same as usual and even the Red Sox hat resembles a crown. Robbie drives like he is driving the Queen of England, and as he turns up the classical music on the radio I know that we will arrive at Fenway Park and home again safely.

The thing about going with Granny to Fenway Park is that she doesn't sit there like the rest of us watching the game. In fact, she only watches the game half of the time because the other half of the time she's looking down at the page in the program that has all of the boxes that she fills out during the entire game. She fills out these boxes using a pen that is the kind of pen that smudges as she writes, so the bottom part of her hand turns darker blue over the course of the game. Granny looks up with every pitch and she makes some sort of note on the box every time there is a strike or a ball or a hit or a home run, which doesn't happen often, but it is always exciting when it does. She uses numbers sometimes, and that isn't as interesting as when she colors in the boxes using diagonal lines to make triangles that she sometimes fills in all the way. Granny focuses so hard on filling out the boxes the right way that she sometimes tells us to be quiet while not using her words.

Another thing about going to Fenway Park with Granny is that we sit in the same seats every time. This means that we see the same people each time and that also means the two ladies with voices that sound like men. These two ladies have sat behind us ever since the first time I went to see a Red Sox game with Granny. They have probably been there for years before also, because one time I heard Granny tell Robbie that she has had these seats in our family ever since after The War, which I imagine happened a long time ago because there has certainly not been a war here since before I was born, which was I think a very long time ago.

These two ladies are so rude! They use swear words and they yell and shout at the players like their voices are the only ones that matter in the entire ballpark. They say things like, "Throw him out, ya bum!" and "C'mon Boggs, hit the goddamned ball!" They kind of yell in order with each other, one after the other, and I think that they might be sisters. They certainly sound exactly alike. They might even be twins. In every game I've ever been to Granny never mentions their filthy language or their smoking during the entire game. I know she must be irritated by them, but I also know that she picks her battles and focuses only on winning the wars. These ladies are not battles to be won, so Granny instead focuses on her scoring and keeping me and my brothers well fed on Fenway Franks and Coke. The only time

144

Sprite tastes better than Fenway Park is on *Windsong* with Dad.

During this game, as the ladies yell like they always do, Robbie snaps, and whips his head around and asks them would they please keep it down? He is here with his grandmother and his sister. The two ladies must have had a conniption inside because they look at each other, then back at Robbie with a look so flat, and as one of them was opening her mouth and raising her finger to point at him, Granny places her arm on Robbie's shoulder and says to him not to worry. They have been sharing this area of Fenway Park for decades and that stands for something. She tells him not to get upset on her account and that she's sure I would agree. I find myself nodding but looking at the ground. Robbie turns around and concentrates on the action in front of us, his forehead wrinkled in a way that, like his eyes in the rear-view mirror, make me think of Dad.

Vicki taught Robbie how to drive. Dad was busy with the store and Mom was going to the twins' hockey practices at five in the morning so she was exhausted all the time. That left Robbie to learn to drive with Vicki and that made a lot of sense because they have always had a good time together. Vicki is my friend, but she's also Robbie's friend and this is true when they go on walks together around Lake Waban, when she takes him to a concert at the college, and when they sit on the porch and talk about school and other things for a long time.

Vicki is still smiling and happy all the time except when she's with Paula who seems to bring out the other parts of her personality that are also important even though they are not as joyful. It is always fun to watch the twins still light up with excitement when Vicki shows up at the house. Kenny especially seems like he drops everything to sit down at the kitchen table and hold hands with everyone around the table and have Vicki lead the chant, "How happy we are, how *happy* we *are*!" We have been doing this since we were little kids and it still brings smiles to our faces. I think that is what Vicki is known for. She has a way of making anyone feel *happy* and she's able to change our minds to focusing on who we *are* instead of who we think we should be.

The one time I saw Vicki lose her temper was when the twins and Robbie were shooting baskets in the driveway and Vicki must have been on the terrace because she wasn't in the house when Robbie said the word he said.

They were shooting baskets when Kenny missed the net several times and Robbie said something that made Vicki come running out from wherever she was (and I really do think it was the terrace) and she came running out from the terrace and she ran so fast and her face was red and her eyes were squinted from running out from the terrace or maybe something else and her arms were thrusting and her feet were kicking up mud and her hair was flying behind her and her body was jiggling but solid at the same time because she had never been so strong as when she ran out from the terrace in such a wild fury that made Kenny drop the ball in his hands so the ball was dropping and Danny and Kenny and Robbie stood frozen as Vicki ran out from the terrace in a red-faced, squinty-eyed, solid yet jiggling body and arms sharp like knives cutting through the air at bent elbows and her voice.

And her voice. Her voice. Not her voice. It was— It hurt. It was crying. It was hard. It hurt. It was her heart-voice and her heart was broken. It hurt. It cut us like a thousand splinters. It was crying. It wailed and it yelled and it cut and it froze. It hurt. It wasn't her voice. And it was. And it was. And it was. It absolutely was.

"And you, Robbie. You are using that word?"

And that was it. That was what made Robbie stutter through his trembles and clog his voice because what he was trying to say had no chance of surviving the sheer force of Vicki's anger. "You are using that word?"

"You?"

"Robbie?"

"That?"

"Word?"

After Robbie fled the scene for somewhere, maybe even the roof, Vicki stood like a statue among the twin statues in front of her. It was like the Wild West when the two cowboys stood like statues across from each other with hands above the guns in their belts. It was exactly like that because the feeling was the same. Tense and crackling with dark electricity coming from someone who up until that moment was the warmth and light of the sun, but here she was standing in front of us as stone-like as the objects at the Museum of Fine Arts with even the warmth of her dripping tears unable to crack the frozen skin on her surface. This wasn't a moment to be proud of, I thought to myself. Yet I was watching someone act out her pride in a way that made me feel more safe than ever before in my life. I knew from that moment that Vicki drew a line of behavior and I knew from that moment that crossing the line would always come to this. And that would not be the end of it.

An hour or so later, I was seeing Vicki and Robbie sitting on the front porch together, with Vicki guiding Robbie's hand on the throat of the guitar and singing with him as he learned the right notes because he already knew the words by heart. They both sang the words together in one unified voice.

>*The water is wide, I cannot get o'er*
>*Neither have I wings to fly*
>*Give me a boat that can carry two*
>*And both shall cross my true love and I*

Is There Something I Should Know?

This one is a doozy.

I'm sitting on the top of the stairs listening to a war happening downstairs. As I rock with my eyes squinted closed, I circle again and again to what I know has happened so far. Something about the store. It's a machine that Dad wanted to buy and he bought and Mom is now throwing everything at him including the kitchen sink. Dad says he needs the machine in order to make the store better. Mom says what the store needs is for him to be some-word-I've-never-heard-before responsible. This is a different-word-I've-never-heard-before she says. They continue on and on using different-words-I've-never-heard-before but I still understand that this war began at the store and it continued on their way home from work in Mom's car because Robbie was driving Dad's car. And it continued on the battlefield at home. The first shot was the back door slamming. That back-door slam was heard around the house and it made me raise my head from my pad of letters and Kenny and Danny were all too happy to stop doing their homework and we silently met on the top of the stairs together, which is where we always meet in order to report on the latest series of events.

Without Robbie there to tell us what's really going on, the

twins and I are left to figure it out without his older brother intelligence. It's okay, though, because Kenny is becoming very good at listening to their words and making the words-I've-never-heard-before seem more understandable. Danny sits silently, which is unusual for such a talkative brother. Neither of them are interested in making me feel better except in order to help me understand what Mom and Dad are at war about. But it's all right because I feel better even though they're not trying to help because just having one twin on one side and the other on the other side is a strong feeling. I wonder how other special sisters in the world manage without two younger brothers to be like bookends when there is a war going on downstairs.

At one point, the noise downstairs gets so loud that I want to take my fist and clench it in front of my face like I used to do. I raise my arm and Kenny takes my wrist with the most gentle force, looks me in the eyes, and says gently, "You don't need to do this any more, Claire. We all know by now their fights always end." If Robbie were with us, he would add something like, "and it's always going to be all right," but he isn't with us and I find myself loosening up with Kenny's words to me anyway. I put my fist down and I rub my corduroys up and down before deciding I don't need to do that any more.

Danny says something about how this is as big as the computer fight from when we were kids and that commercial came on television and Dad bought that machine, too. I think to myself that maybe Dad has a machine-buying problem and maybe if he just controls his wallet he and Mom will not get into these huge fights. Or maybe Mom can be in charge of the credit card. Or maybe they could just talk to each other about it before buying the machine. It seems easy to just talk about whatever it is that you want and get the person with the credit card excited about spending it on what you want. But then maybe it's not that easy because I continue to get socks and gloves at Christmas and if it were so easy I would be following my own advice. But I don't, because even though I know what I don't want for Christmas I don't know what I do want. For some reason this is way too complicated for me to understand.

Another bomb goes off downstairs when one of them opens and slams the back door behind them and leaves behind silence but not like the thick blanket kind. This silence sucks something out from my tummy and replaces it with a swarm of moths and my skin tingles like it's covered with spiders. I'm not sure who it was who slammed the back door behind them and got in the station wagon and backed it down the driveway and headed up the hill. My twin brothers look at each other and then at me and they say we should watch television. But that means going downstairs and seeing Mom or Dad still standing in the kitchen because we haven't heard any more footsteps. Just at that moment, there is the sound of Dad clearing his throat and we know it is safe to go downstairs because Dad is always able to put his feelings away after an argument. So we head downstairs and all of us with Dad watch an episode of *The Cosby Show* and Dad laughs especially loudly and reminds me of Mrs. Hinman and the trumpet laugh she does because she isn't really laughing from deep inside.

I'm the first one to see the headlights hit the garage and I know that it is Dad's car because it sounds like an old Volvo not a new station wagon and I'm proven correct when the crunching sound of the parking brake cuts through the dark silence of the night. A few seconds later, I hear the back door open and gently shut.

Robbie's home. I hear the sound of bags shuffling and papers being either put inside or taken out. I'm curious about what Robbie is doing and I walk into the kitchen just as his taller self walks out into the front hall and up the stairs. I always know when Robbie is going up the stairs because of his feet. They stomp "like a runaway elephant", according to Dad.

I feel like it is very important to tell Robbie about what happened tonight, so I shout up the stairs, *Mom and Dad got into a big fight tonight.* I see his boots walk in a hurry across the upstairs hall toward the stairs to his attic room. He is still wearing his overcoat and I wonder why he is in such a hurry when he quickly but clearly says, "Good."

Good?

He mustn't have heard me. So I follow him upstairs and across the upstairs hallway and the door is open a bit to the stairs up to his attic bedroom so I go up the stairs. I find that I'm being careful and quiet and I'm walking slowly up the stairs and I wonder why. The moths in my tummy have decided to fly around at lightning speed so as I slow down they speed up. At the top of the stairs, I look around because I'm not often up in Robbie's room and it is really very interesting. The bathroom door is shut, so I assume he is doing whatever business he needs to do.

The white walls are full of posters from sports cars to rock bands including U2, which I like because I can read their name without any trouble because it is spelled just like it sounds. All three of my brothers love U2. They are rock and roll and they also have something Robbie calls depth. When I think about depth, I think about the blue pool or the Herring River or the ocean when we are on *Windsong.* I guess depth makes me think about summer, not rock bands. There is another band that is the five men and one who wears lipstick. I get closer to them because they are dressed very smart and I think more than one wears make-up and they are all very attractive. Juliet says this is her favorite band because it is Princess Diana's favorite band. I have seen them on MTV recordings Robbie has made on the VCR and their videos are the ones that take place on sailboats much bigger and more colorful than *Windsong*.

His bookshelves are packed with so many books and his desk is an absolute mess with papers and binders and a typewriter and his own phone and a box that I open containing old tickets from U2 concerts, Red Sox games, Bruins games and many more. Near the bottom I see the ticket from *Cats* and I hold it a moment longer than the others and I make sure to put it on the top of the pile now. I don't care if it means Robbie knows I was going through his ticket box. I think he would be interested to know that I was interested in reliving that memory.

I'm distracted by an awful smell that takes me back to Mom and Dad's cocktail parties and Lake Waban. Could it be? I walk to the bathroom door and talk through the slots: *Robbie, are you in there?* There is no reply. *Robbie?* I turn the doorknob and squeak open the door and he isn't in there but the window across from me is open and the screen is neatly resting on the sink counter like it really means something. I find myself whispering Robbie's name but hoping he does not hear me as I peek out the window and look to the side and I see Robbie sitting on the roof facing a different direction than me and in a cloud of smoke that must be refreshing to him because it really is cold outside.

But smoking isn't good for you and I want to tell that to him but I see he is outside in the cold on the roof and quiet and the stars

153

are pricking in the sky and he is telling the world that he needs peace and quiet so I give it to him. This isn't the same as when Greg Brady was caught smoking at high school because he was coughing all the time and it didn't look like it does with Robbie on this freezing night. Tonight Robbie smoking on the roof looks peaceful and right. I know to step away and leave him be.

After closing the bathroom door like it was, and before I walk down the stairs two by two, I open the ticket box on Robbie's desk and I make sure the *Cats* ticket is back on the bottom where it belongs. I know that Robbie would have noticed it on the top and I think he would have cared but it is important to put the old ticket back on the bottom where it belongs.

I Ran

Juliet and I are wearing our Stewed Tomato T-shirts that we picked up from the Stewed Tomato restaurant in Chatham last year. We wear the same kind of white shorts and she wears sneakers and I wear a pair of Velcro sandals that are new because they never used to have Velcro sandals in stores until this year. I swirl my Special K in my skim milk and look at the orange juice in front of me. Juliet hasn't drunk hers, either, and I don't think she wants to. The breeze on the screen porch causes my paper napkin to fly off the table and Juliet picks it up off the floor and hands it to me. It is that kind of a morning. We are waking up to a sleepy house and it is so quiet that I hear the floorboards creaking and the flag flapping and the river lapping the shore in little ripples.

Grandpops walks into the porch and stops and looks at us and asks whether he ever told us the story about him and Brussels sprouts. He thinks I don't like the cereal but I just eat slowly because Juliet eats very slowly and I don't want her to feel like she's holding me up. After he tells me the story I've heard a few times before, I eat another spoonful of Special K and tell him, *I'm fine*. He crinkles his smiling eyes and says, "Good", and shuffles over to his favorite chair in the corner of the porch, snaps open his

155

Cape Cod Times and starts reading, humming to himself. I know that it won't take long before I forget he is there. After a moment, Juliet removes her eyes from him and back down to her bowl of cereal. If I listen carefully, I think I hear her humming, too. This means she's happy here, and I'm happy too.

Our bowls now empty, Juliet asks where the twins and Robbie are. I tell her they are at sailing school and that Robbie is a counselor at Becket, his overnight camp. She asks when Mom and Dad are coming back. I say when the printing store is closed and they can join us. She makes a noise and nods and moves her wide eyes toward the river. As she stares out to the river, I take my orange juice quickly in three gulps. When Gammy enters the porch and sees our empty plates and glasses, she appears satisfied. She asks how much longer we will stay on the porch and whether we are planning to spend all day there. Juliet looks at me while I wonder how to respond because of course we are not going to stay here at the table all day. That would be a waste of time. I think that was her way of reminding me that there are things to do that can't be done by just sitting on the porch. I think about Grandpops, still sitting on the porch, reading every page of the *Cape Cod Times*, including the comics, like he has all the time in the world.

This peaceful moment is rudely interrupted by the buzz of a speedboat that cuts through the river's mirror-like surface. You never see Grandpops jump out of his porch chair more quickly than when a boat goes faster than the speed limit on the river. Before we know it, Grandpops is standing on the end of our dock, his Hawaiian shirt showing that he is relaxed and has vacation on his mind but his flailing arms reminding everyone that he hasn't forgotten the rules of the river. He shouts, "Slow down!", and the people on the boat race by. He yells something else as the driver of the boat turns his head to look at him through his cool sunglasses under his white visor. I can't hear what Grandpops says, but whatever it was seems to have done the trick because the boat slows down in a rush of water that pushes it over its own waves. The cool boat driver waves back at Grandpops, who gives him an opposite-wave back, like he is shooing away a swarm of mosquitoes. Grandpops shuffles back to the porch, muttering to himself the whole way until he is settled back in his porch chair with his *Cape Cod Times* open in front of him and before we know it he is humming to himself like nothing happened.

Driving to pick up the twins from the yacht club is always quite an experience with Gammy and Grandpops. They both have the same type of old car. They are long and wide and low to the ground with hot leather seats that Juliet and I need a towel to sit on. They have a radio where you need to push the button in hard in order to get the station and there is usually static. The windows need you to be strong in order to open because they are big windows that you have to crank hard in order to open and shut just like Dad's old Volvo with the Bruins trophy hanging from the sunroof handle. The cars are like Gammy and Grandpops because they are stronger than you think they should be and the staticky radio is how they sound sometimes but when you listen carefully you find that it is true.

Juliet stares out the window at nothing in particular. "Clear to port," says Grandpops, as he drives. "Clear to starboard," says Gammy, as Grandpops makes the turn onto the busy street. His car seat makes him appear very small, and he tilts his chin up in order to look above the steering wheel. He keeps both of his hands on the wheel and he doesn't say anything on the entire journey except when it is clear and then Gammy responds when it is clear on her side. I think she tells him about the clear to starboard side because if Grandpops turned his head that way it would be straining his neck and it would feel tight and maybe hurt. I like how they work together as they drive in the same car because they appear like one person, which is sometimes how the twins are and sometimes how I think Juliet and I are. When Gammy and Grandpops appear like one person in the car, I feel safe to listen to Gammy talk through the static of the engine and the wind rushing through the windows and the squeaks of the hot leather seats.

"I just don't understand. They never look happy." Gammy says this when we pass by a woman jogging down the street facing us. She is right, the woman does not look happy and in fact she looks like she's in pain. But exercise isn't easy and at least she's outside in the sun and getting healthy. Gammy continues talking about the jogger until she has long passed us. She does not know why especially women are not happy just walking quickly or even just riding a bike. Running is hard on the knees and besides, why do women feel the need to get strong like a man? She continues talking to no one in particular because Grandpops is driving with both hands on the wheel. As we pull into the gravelly yacht club parking lot and I see the twins sitting on the wall talking with another boy and holding their orange life preservers, Gammy says something that cuts through the static of the rest of the journey. "It looks like these joggers are all being chased. Like they are running away from something, but there's really nothing chasing after them at all."

*

158

My family's communication with Robbie this summer is through letters. For two months we haven't seen him but we read letters he writes from Becket. I always look forward to his letters because they would be about the funny things the little kids in his cabin are doing. When Robbie left, he told us that he was excited to finally be a counselor and that he expects that this summer will be a very important summer for him while we do the regular stuff we usually do here on the Cape. I think Mom and Dad were smart to have Juliet with us this summer because the twins have each other and there is no Robbie to hang out with.

We sit at the dining room table that makes one side look short and the other look tall because the floor is lopsided because it's such an old house. When Robbie enters, I can barely recognize him because he has grown even more and his hair has turned very light blonde and he smiles so brightly that I forgot he had got his braces off just before going off to Becket two months ago. When he walks into the house, we all get up and Mom gives him a huge hug and Dad comes over and shakes his hand while the twins give him a wave from where they sit at the table. There is a glow around him that tells me he has grown a lot this summer and not just in height. He could be a soldier home from war and I wouldn't know the difference. That is how much closer he is now between boy and man.

I look over at Juliet and her face doesn't lie. When Robbie comes over to her, the only person who did not stand up when he entered, she gets up like a rocket and he hugs her. As he hugs her, she doesn't let go. Juliet's crush on Robbie began that night and I don't think it has ever really gone away. Once everything has settled down, Robbie sits in the empty chair and starts reaching for the bowl of potatoes and the salad. As Dad passes over the platter of steak that he prepared just right, Robbie holds up his hand, saying he is a vegetarian now and that he is dating a girl from New Jersey named Doreen whom he met at the girls' camp. Doreen is a vegetarian, too. And she's really very cool and someday we will all meet her. Juliet stares at her plate, as if in a trance, yet I know exactly what she's thinking and that is okay. We will talk about it later tonight, when we always talk about what needs talking about, without words, just sharing our thoughts as we drift off to sleep.

"You know what, Claire? I thought I would have a hard time being patient with the kids but instead I worry that I was too easy on them. They were awesome!" As he stretches on the front lawn in his running clothes, Robbie talks to me and Juliet all about Becket and the time he had there this summer. Juliet and I are sitting in our lawn chairs with our Sprites in plastic glasses with ice and wearing our Stewed Tomato T-shirts again. Juliet wears sunglasses but I don't because they make me uncomfortable, like jewelry and hair stuff. I wonder if Juliet is wearing sunglasses for other reasons not to do with the sun. She stays fully silent the entire time Robbie stretches and I wonder what must be going through her head because if she was bored she would be nodding off to sleep by now. I know her well.

Robbie leaps to his feet and puts the yellow headphones in his ears and carries his Walkman in his right hand. He waves goodbye to us, and Juliet makes the first movement since plopping herself in the lawn chair when she waves goodbye to Robbie. As we watch him disappear behind the trees as he heads down the driveway, I think about how he is running every day like he has since he was in ninth grade. He runs and runs and runs so that when I think about what Gammy said about the jogger I think about Robbie and what he might be running from and whether maybe he is different because he might just enjoy running for its own sake. Yes, that must be it. He runs because he loves to run and it makes him feel good. I look at Juliet, who is nodding off in the lawn chair, completely relaxed. I hear the twins on the tennis court fighting about whether it was in or out. I hear Mom talking to Gammy through the open kitchen window and I hear the whaler engine starting with Dad and Grandpops behind the wheel. Yes, I'm sure he runs because he enjoys it. Just because I don't doesn't mean he shouldn't. If it makes him happy, I won't question it. His last year of high school is coming up, and I need to be supportive of him because soon he will be away for much longer than just two months.

Pulling Mussels (from the Shell)

Juliet and I are painting the seashells we collected at Skaket Beach. Skaket Beach is a special place because it isn't like any other beach on the Cape because there are no waves and sometimes the water is so far out that we can walk on wet sand for what feels like miles. When we walk, our toes get tickled by minnows that are stuck in the little pools. There are crabs, but they are very small and definitely no blue claws that can cut your big toe off. There are no jellyfish in the water and the best thing is that there are no waves.

We walk out with our plastic buckets with numb lips and the bitter taste of suntan lotion on tongues. It is a heat wave right now, so we wear suntan lotion all the time and it irritates me because of how I hate having stuff like that on my skin. It is better than getting a sunburn, though. Shell collecting is one of the things Juliet does very fast. For someone who is slow to move, to eat, and to wake up in the morning, she collects shells like our new puppy, Cody, searching for tennis balls behind the court.

But watch her go! Once we head toward the water, she's off and running and bending over to collect whatever she can see. When Juliet collects seashells, she takes all of the ones that look good, and she rinses them, and she tosses out most of them after a second look. Her big, round sunglasses that cover most of her face help her see the shells without needing to squint out the glare of the sunlight. They also add a glamorous look to her, especially with her beach hat, which is a wide, floppy thing that bends in the breeze when there is a breeze. But today there is no breeze at all and I feel the sun eating away at my greasy skin like the fire ants who used to eat my feet while I was waiting for a half an hour to pass before swimming at Morningside Day Camp.

Back on the porch, we are deeply focused on creating art from the ocean. Our plastic buckets are full of white, pink, gray, blue and tan shells eager to be painted in colors they wouldn't imagine in their wildest dreams. We have covered the table in a plastic tablecloth and we have our sets of watercolor paints open and our plastic water cups are filled with our paintbrushes inside, becoming clean after use. Our finished works of art sit on paper towels to dry. Something happens when we paint seashells. We each have our plastic buckets filled to the rim with them. It looks like we will never get through them all. But all of a sudden we are the new owners of a hundred colored seashells that look so much nicer because they have been painted with all sorts of patterns that we created. I never remember the painting part even though it takes three hours according to the clock on the porch.

I also feel like I learn more about Juliet during our time painting the seashells. We talk using words sometimes but mostly not using words at all. When Gammy comes in and listens to her symphony music on her staticky radio, we don't notice because it seems to turn into the air around us. The music fades away but our conversation turns up the volume between us. The conversation is never something worth repeating because it is impossible for me to remember the words we use with each other. But after three or more hours fly by, I feel like Juliet is more known to me than before our painting and it makes me think about how the Cape is special for conversations like this that make best friends feel even closer. I think about this as I look out at the silently flowing river, listen to the welcome late afternoon breeze and inhale the salty air that heightens the feelings of everything from smells like the low tide to sounds like the flag flapping to conversations both spoken and unspoken to best friendships like mine with Juliet.

"Whose brilliant idea was this, anyway?" Robbie, from the bow of *Windsong*, asks anyone who might be listening. I'm holding the salt and vinegar Cape Cod Potato Chips under the shade of the catboat's very large sail. Danny is next to me, playing games by reaching into the bag when I'm not looking. Dad is at the Captain's Wheel and Kenny sits across from Danny and me, drinking his Coke from a can and looking out for whatever he can see on the surface of this flat, dead, endless ocean. Robbie continues his rant, observing that there are no other boats out here except for us and that anyone with any common sense would not have powered out from the mouth of the river just to sit here like a bathtub in the middle of a lake of nothingness. Somehow I remember the bathtub comparison because it is so unusual, so exact, so Robbie.

Dad falls for the bait as he responds, giving some answer like we all need to experience different weather conditions. Robbie attacks with sharp words I don't remember but can still feel. The tension in the cockpit is strong with silence. I can hear Danny crunching his chips, Kenny's fizzy drink, Dad's wheel squeaking as he attempts to make this big bathtub of a boat move even just a bit. Juliet, napping in the cabin, is the only person on board who is content. I wish I were asleep right now because I'm tired from the heat and tired of the company. I wish Robbie would relax a bit. I don't understand why he is so temperamental ever since getting back from Becket but boy is he moody and boy can we all feel it.

The air is thick with humidity and everyone is sweating on their forehead except for Juliet. Even Dad looks like he could use a shower, and I wish I were still on the porch painting the sea shells all safe and sound and with ice at our beck and call. The boat really does feel heavy on the water, and it is true that we are the only thing out here except for floating jellyfish, which seem to have multiplied this year from years past.

Robbie stands up, looks at us, and says, "If you can't take the heat, get in the water!" and jumps in. Before Dad says what's on his mind, Danny follows Robbie by doing a very impressive dive into the ocean and he emerges with his characteristically toothy grin. Kenny looks at Dad, who shrugs, and jumps in. Dad looks at me, and I know exactly what he is about to say. *No, I'm fine.* Then the chorus from the ocean loudly calls me to join them. I shake my head and try to change the subject. *Watch out for jellyfish! Kenny, you just ate potato chips… Don't get a cramp! Be quiet – Juliet's taking a nap.* They aren't having any of it. Dad zips up my life jacket and unfolds the ladder, gesturing with his open hand for me to walk down into the water. I look over at my brothers' heads bobbing in the shimmering sunlight and decide to make them happy. Besides, Juliet sleeps like a log. There is no way we will wake her up.

While in the water, I bob around, looking at my brothers with their hair slicked back and diving for shells from the bottom of the shallow water. The boat towers over me, and sometimes it seems that it might run me over. Dad has tossed out a rope in case we start floating away and I see the sandy beach not too far away from us.

At this moment, I feel like I could actually swim over to that beach if I had to, like if I really did start floating away. At this moment, I hear the seal-like yelps from my twin brothers and the deeper sea-lion roars of my brother Robbie and I remember how when they were younger I thought the twins were just like otters. There is no time passed between back then and today. The twins may as well be five years old all over again by the way they frolic, dip and dive into the bathwaters of the Cape. I'm safe and sound, in my life jacket with a rope to grab and no current or waves to get in my way of having a good time. Dad watches with his camera in one hand and his Heineken in another, grinning ear to ear with a smile looking very much like the smile on Robbie's face as he bobs and basks in the salty water, eager for his own baptism by the ocean that has taken him and all of us into its vast thickness for as long as we can remember.

We hear the distant sound of rackets hitting tennis balls and decide to bring Kenny and Danny a treat to cool them down after such a hot day. I'm glad they waited until now to play tennis because now it is cooler and they won't pass out from heatstroke. We fill a water pitcher with ice and water from the faucet. Juliet asks whether they want cucumber in the water because it makes the water even more thirst-quenching. I have never heard of such a thing, but I trust Juliet to know the right thing to do so I hand her a cucumber from the refrigerator and she gets chopping. From the sink window I can see the twins through the trees. They are looking like the tennis players we watched on television earlier this summer. Both of them are growing and they will soon be starting high school and they will get busier with their schoolwork like Robbie did when he started high school.

Moments later, we are sitting in the outdoor chairs and the tray with the water pitcher and the glasses is on the table between us. We picked two glasses that the twins would like. One is a plastic glass with a tennis player whose racket has a hole from a tennis ball hit through it. It is a funny cartoon. The other is a glass that has US Open 1987 on it. It makes me think about the time when Dad took the twins to see the tennis in New York. I remember the twins coming back and unable to stop speaking about Lendl, Connors, and the human temper tantrum John McEnroe who failed to disappoint, according to Dad. I remember wondering if his temper was the same as Jed's. After watching him on television, I decided they must be related.

We are both amazed at the level of tennis talent the twins have. Kenny's serve is like lightning and Danny is light on his feet and he returns the serve most of the time. They both play up near the net so they hit the ball without it bouncing and I chuckle because at least the ball isn't going through the racket like it does on the plastic glass. They don't seem dizzy or like they might trip on their feet like I would. They seem connected so when Kenny is on the back left, Danny is on the front right. They move this way, and if we removed the rackets it would seem as if they are in a dance together. Light on their feet, well balanced and rhythmic. Maybe it's because they are twins.

Mom and Dad join them for doubles. This is my favorite part about watching tennis at the Cape. It used to be even better when Gammy and Grandpops would also play but that was a long time ago and now they are older. Mom and Dad play with their wooden rackets, which they have always played with. Mom's two-handed backhand is powerful! Kenny has a hard time returning it. Dad has a beautiful serve and it looks like ballet.

My pride in them swells inside. Tennis is certainly not something I could even begin to do. Yet as Juliet says, it is more fun to watch because we don't get sweaty or tired or frustrated when the ball is out or argumentative when it is on the line. Yes, all of that is a hassle. Still, sometimes I have dreams when I can play tennis like my family and it feels wondrous to be light on my feet, well balanced and rhythmic. It is hard to wake up from those dreams but I soon forget them by the time I sit down for breakfast.

too many people so I don't get embarrassed. But I will be seen and Kenny will take pictures from the sidelines and everyone will smile and be proud of me. I'm the first one to finish school completely. Robbie will be next, then the twins. This is the beginning of something new for all of us. Tomorrow, I will have a diploma on my wall, just like everyone does when they graduate. Today, I just need to get the diploma, smile, say "Thank you", and eat without spilling on my white dress.

Well, that was quick. Last Friday I graduated from St Coletta's and Kenny took some really nice pictures, especially because he was allowed to be with the other photographers who had big black lenses so he had the best view of anyone and it shows in the pictures. He spent the rest of the day developing his favorites and no one saw him until breakfast the next day. At breakfast, he shared a pile of pictures from my graduation day. I think that even though they were black and white, the colors of the day still came through. At least the glows off everyone's faces certainly did. It was a beautiful day, so the sunlight reflected really nicely. Yet even Gammy looked younger and genuinely happy. And Robbie and his girlfriend and my brothers. Oh, and Mom! She glowed in the black and white as much as she did in my favorite picture of her from her fortieth birthday on the Cape. I was eleven, Robbie was nine, the twins were six. And Mom was forty. And her tan, and her blue dress, her white teeth that were bright with genuine happiness, and her glow that came from something else entirely all give this picture a million years to live before turning yellow and fading away.

I sit on the radiator waiting for the van and it pulls in just on time at 8:40 because it is now 8:40 when the van arrives, and that gives me more time to sleep in, which is great because who doesn't want to sleep in every morning? The van arrives and Mom comes out with me to meet the driver and suddenly she exclaims, "Claire! Come over and see who your new van driver is!" I walk around to the driver's side and immediately see that he's not a new van driver. He is my old van driver, Mike! Mike actually gets out of the van to give me a hug. He smells just the same. He looks just the same. Everything is going to be the same even though the people and the routines will be different. Mike asks where Sandy is and we introduce him to Cody who still jumps around with a puppy's hollow bones and rubber feet. He and Mom have a bit more small talk about the printing store, about where my brothers are now in school, and about how nice the landscaping looks. By the time they are done talking, Mom looks around for me and even yells my name as if I'm back in the house but I'm already in the van, seatbelt in, ready to get going to my new job and to meet my new co-workers and to try out my new routine.

This biggest difference between school and my new job is that in my new job I'm surrounded by people who all need assistance with things not just learning but going to the bathroom and eating and having their clothes washed and folded. That is my job in the hospital. I wash and fold the patients' clothes and bed sheets and napkins. The patients are very happy that I do this because clean clothes and bed sheets and napkins are important. My director, Margarita, tells me that this isn't even about being clean. It is about giving these people dignity.

Dignity is what it feels like when you have clean clothes and you're eating with clean napkins. It is what it feels like when someone has taken time to make something nice for you so that

172

you can look the best you can and people will think wow this person has it all together. The clean napkins are about dignity because you put napkins on your mouth and they should be clean, of course. The clean bed sheets mean that you have somewhere to look forward to going at the end of your day. You have a bed that will take you in without germs or dirt or worse and it will guarantee a pleasant sleep with sweet dreams.

My favorite part of the day is lunch in the cafeteria. Margarita and I ate together the first few days and she would ask me all sorts of questions with a clipboard and a pen that was putting checks in boxes and her glasses on the tip of her nose. I understand this is what she has to do for her job and to make sure that I'm comfortable here. She doesn't tell me much about herself, and I don't tell her much about me because that isn't the kind of person I am and also I think it is her job to ask the questions about my life. So I don't share and neither does she but it still feels fine. Each day we have lunch, other people want to join us and they all seem excited to meet me. "Claire or Clarissa? *No, I'm Claire.* "Do you live in Newton?" *No.* "How long have you been here?" *Three days. Since Monday.*

"What is your favorite food?" That gets my attention. I look up and meet Joyce, a nurse who seems to have something different about her. *Pizza with pepperoni.* "Color?" *I don't have one but my brothers' are red, blue and green.* "What did you eat for breakfast this morning?" *Special K with bananas. And orange juice.* I always forget to drink my orange juice. "How do you get here?" *With my van driver, Mike.* "Has your hair always been that pretty?" *Thank you very much.* Margarita is another reason my new work is different from school. That song from Annie with the tight perm is in my head and on repeat for the entire rest of the day.

173

I think I'm gonna like it here...

When I really think about it, my job means a lot to people and I make people feel dignity like they should. Like everyone should. Even the smoker in the bathroom at St Coletta's who I know doesn't have clean clothes and probably doesn't wipe her face with clean napkins. Remembering how dark and tired her eyes were, I don't think she had a clean bed to tuck into every night and I doubt very much that she had a pleasant sleep with sweet dreams at night. And I know that she never had a friend at school like I have in Margarita. Margarita the nurse. Margarita the one with the questions. Margarita the person who greets me in the morning with a huge wave from across the laundry room. Margarita the sunshine of my day because if I can't have Vicki with me, I could do a lot worse than have Margarita. And I think she feels the same about me, which feels like dignity, doesn't it?

Holiday

Every Saturday I go to Parkland Rec, which is in Natick and not too far away from my town. When I go to Parkland Rec, I do all sorts of activities. There is Zumba class, there is painting and sculpting, there is yoga and there is even swimming because Parkland Rec has a huge pool that people use to swim long laps and dive from the high diving boards. One time I saw a diver who arched his back like Danny does when he serves on the tennis court. He dove and spun and entered the water without even a splash. The sound was more like a zip. And it was beautiful. Like Greg Louganis beautiful. I remember Greg Louganis because during the Summer Olympics a few years ago he was diving off the high diving board and he was like a dolphin in the air. Until he hit his head and it bled and he had to leave the pool with stitches. Robbie was the most upset about this because he felt like no one who works so hard for something like diving should have to deal with a setback like that. He was going through his why bad things happen to good people phase when he kept talking at the dinner table about the Morningside Day Camp counselor who died in the plane explosion over Scotland. I remember her. She wore sunglasses and taught swimming and she was nice like Sally. Greg Louganis did not deserve to bump his head on that diving board. He did not deserve to wince in pain and hear the gasps and face the wall of silence afterwards. When Greg Louganis walked away from the pool he was as if his glow was sucked out through his heart and into the air, gone for good.

When I think about bad things happening to good people, I think about when Robbie can't print his essay or when Kenny loses his camera lens or when Danny can't win over the girl by his shiny smile alone. I think about when Mom and Dad's printing store doesn't post a profit (as Dad sometimes calls it) and when Granny burns the leftovers. When Gammy's tomatoes get eaten by the mysterious fox or when Grandpops can't mow the lawn anymore because of his arthritis. There are people who are bent because they are overloaded with questions. There are people who have spiral eyes because they try to understand why bad things happen to them while they continue to move through their days. These are the people whose eyes spiral like the cartoons when they can't see straight and clear. These are the people whose spiral eyes are laced with sadness because they have hit their tipping point and they just need to cut a break. They are in church, they are in the supermarket, they are at our porch cocktail parties wearing colorful summer dresses that can't disguise their dark and confused hearts. They are living the song Robbie likes called "Mad World". They are pushing through their days on low batteries, causing their light to flicker and be brown like when we are about to have a blackout.

When Kate sees people like this wandering the aisles in CVS like ghosts, she tells me she doesn't get it. She tells me she would understand if they were all dealing with a tragedy. And maybe they are, I say. She agrees that yes, they might be, and tragedy might lead everyone to CVS pharmacy to wander the aisles. And

176

if that is so, then her job is more important that she thought. It's like she's cleaning the aisles of the sanctuary at church. She is cleaning a place that people go to to feel better about themselves and about their lives.

But Kate says that a lot of the time people come in and they have an edge like just one accidental bump into them or one question about where is the toothpaste or one sneeze in their general direction might cause an explosive reaction. It is these people who Kate says should not be in CVS or any store. They should just be home and figure out what it is that makes them edgy and quick to explode. If they did this, Kate says, they could then leave their houses with dignity and a glow again. Surely it shouldn't take much time to figure out that you're upset about the burnt toast or the angry boss or the teenage son with a piss-poor attitude. But once outside of the house, Kate reminds me, we are on display in front of the world. And that matters because we can make other people feel good or bad or angry or joyful by what we carry with us when we leave the house. And I'm not talking about a purse or backpack or baby in a sling.

When Kate gets very excited about something, she gets loud like normally people do but because of her weak throat she also drools out the side of her mouth. When she usually drools, she wipes it away as soon as it appears to drip down to her chin. But when she's very excited, it is like she doesn't feel it or she just forgets about it because what she's saying is much more important than whatever is dripping down the side of her face because of her weak throat. When Donna gets excited about something, she moves her wheelchair back and forth really quickly, almost like it is keeping rhythm with her heartbeat. Or maybe she is bumping into the toes of the person she's talking to in order to make sure he is still paying attention to her. When Dwight gets excited, he stands very close to your face and his voice gets higher and his arms move in big motions like he is drawing circles with his hands. When Christine gets excited, she doesn't change at all. Her voice is always at a low volume and every word sounds exactly the same. With Christine it is like the poster of the bald eagle staring at the camera and underneath it says, "I AM smiling."

This is almost as good as the goat that is so behind he thinks he is first. Sometimes the people who walk into CVS for no reason but because they have spiral eyes and dark hearts are also far behind but they also seem to think they are first. That baffles me but I let it go because why waste energy on questions that circle in our minds like Dwight's hands in the air?

The television tells us to forget our troubles and go on a Disney Cruise. So that is where I'm heading. My group from Parkland Rec is going to be on a Disney Cruise for five days and we will have so much fun! Dwight's younger sister Suzie is coming also because now that she's in college she can do these things. I like being with Suzie because she's wonderful and her laugh is deep. She is also someone I think is organized and if my friends or I get lost or something she will find us before we even know we are lost. That is what makes Suzie so good to be around. It is funny because growing up I always just thought of her as Dwight's little sister but now I look up to her and I know that she has grown up so much.

On the huge ship we run into Goofy and Mickey and Donald Duck and the others and it feels funny because we are not kids but we think it is nice to have them on board, too. The regular people are so nice. They help with everything like showing where the elevators and ramps are for people like Donna. They show Kate where the EpiPens are kept and they always know where the nearest bathroom is. With Suzie and Drew as our leaders, and with the nice regular people on the ship who are not dressed up like cartoon people, we feel comfortable and able to relax and order frozen daiquiris on the pool deck.

My eyes are closed while wearing sunglasses that Suzie gave me because she thinks they will feel good on my face and not irritate me like the other sunglasses always do. So far she's right. These sunglasses are red and plastic and so lightweight it doesn't feel like they are even on my face. They say Disney in yellow cursive on the sides and I don't mind that because from now on I think that word will mean something different to me than just cartoons. With my eyes closed while wearing sunglasses, I listen to everything I possibly can. There is a Marco Polo game at the far end of the pool. There is a couple of people playing catch with a beach ball close to me but I'm not worried because even if the ball hits me it is just a beach ball and I know they are like feathers. There are some people listening to a story being told on a radio and I think they might be blind because I saw them come to the pool deck in a line following the leader with the radio. There are a lot of giggles and laughs and the smells are enough to keep my tummy rumbling all day long. I'm sure Dwight is taking advantage of the endless hot dogs. His parents would not be pleased but Suzie is here and I'm sure she's keeping an extra eye on him.

Even while lying here with my eyes closed and my sunglasses on I still feel that feeling like someone is looking at me. Sometimes that happens to me. Like at a dance when it is dark but I know someone is watching me. Or even in the light it is amazing how you can tell someone is watching you from across the river when you can't possibly look into their eyes. So I open my eyes because I know whoever is watching me can't tell my eyes are open thanks to the sunglasses.

I'm glad I opened my eyes behind my sunglasses! The first thing I notice is that he is so tall. So very, very tall. A giant. And he has a gentle face. It isn't pinched like the people who walk into CVS carrying their dark hearts and spiral eyes. This man is kind I can tell and he is stuck in a stare and I begin to feel bad because I know he is stuck in a stare with me and I know this. So I take off my sunglasses. They were beginning to make my nose sweat anyway. As I look around me, Christine, with her *People* magazine open on her thighs and without lifting her eyes from the pictures, says, "He's been watching you all morning." I don't say anything. I squirm a bit while figuring out what to do. I get up, and walk toward the bar to get myself a Sprite with ice.

The giant arrives just ahead of me and that is when the magic begins. He orders my Sprite for me and shows his ID number on the tag around his neck so they know to charge him and not me. He talks about life in South Carolina where he is from. He says he has an older brother and two younger sisters. He goes to church and his mother is sick. His father is his role model and they watch Formula One together. His favorite movie is *Star Wars* and he is a huge fan of The Boss and the LA Lakers. "Oh, I'm talking way too much. Tell me about you. What do you like?"

Swimming and the Cape and my friends who are all here on this Disney Cruise. Pizza and dogs that catch tennis balls and drawing on a pad in my room. My van driver Mike and walking around Lake Waban with Vicki. I go to Village Church and Mr.

Gallagher who has shaky hands treats me kindly. My parents are nice and my brothers care about me very much even though they are getting older and Robbie is away in college. I graduated from St. Coletta's last year and I love my job at the hospital because it is good to clean things people use every day when they are too busy getting healthy to do it themselves. I don't tell him that my last boyfriend was Jed and that we broke up several years ago.

After who knows how long, Donna wheels up to us and asks the bartender for a Cherry Coke with extra cherry and without missing a beat asks us, "So when is the wedding?" At that moment, watching George's face turn red underneath his sunburn, I realize that her question does not seem as crazy as it sounds. His eyes tell me he is thinking the same thing and at that point I welcome all the dizziness washing over me like waves that build up and cast off the back of the ship.

The rest of the cruise is a blur except for George who is crystal clear and as Kenny would say "in sharp focus". We walk around the deck in the morning, at sunset, and under the stars after dinner. We swim in the pool and when he holds my back as I try to float I can barely feel his fingertips. I watch him shoot hoops for a long time because it is his favorite thing to do. We eat a lot of food and we drink a lot of Sprite. I don't think he was a big Sprite drinker before meeting me. We play arcade games and we sit next to each other at *Sheer Madness* and our knees touch and stay that way the whole performance. He walks me to my door every night and he gives me a quick kiss on my mouth. A very quick one. Very unlike Jed who kind of messed with my mouth like he was Cody licking the dog bowl. George's kisses are gentle just like he is.

I enter my bedroom as Kate is giving herself the pink medicine from a medicine dropper. Even while her tongue is out to get the drops, I can understand what she's saying. Things like how she likes George and that good things come to those who wait. Things like even though he is a giant, he is a gentle giant and those are the best giants because they are always helpful so we can do things we never thought possible beforehand. He speaks quietly and he does not have a temper even when they are behind serving dinner and everyone else is restless with tummies rumbling and asking how they can run out of food when it is supposed to be an endless buffet. I have seen worse, and fortunately on this cruise there was no lawyer shouting I'm suing and no rich people waving their silver credit cards demanding refunds and no spoiled kids tugging at their parents' shirt tails and yelling how miserable and bored and hungry they are and why didn't they go skiing at Vail instead.

No, it was none of that. The Disney cruise is a peaceful success with no fighting and no arguments. Even as roommates, Kate and I never had a bad day. I think we know each other so well by now that any fights are avoided. Kate leaves the bathroom door closed when she uses the bathroom. She keeps the towels on their racks. She sets her alarm clock so it says the same time as my watch. That is still very important to me and Kate knows that it is better to pave the way for me than deal with a freak out that has been known to happen in front of people I love who I know can handle it. I think George could handle it, too. And I think he is someone who would make sure the clocks are set in time to my watch. He is my gentle giant who only wants life to be smooth, calm, and full of opportunities to do things we never thought we could do beforehand.

Dancing with Myself

It is a quiet house. Kenny and Danny are away in France with their school and Mom and Dad are working very hard at the store and I get home at four o'clock and stick to my routine. I walk through the side door and call out for Cody, who stumbles his way down the stairs with his dog collar jingling and his paws tap-tap-tapping on the kitchen floor. The kibble is in the cabinet above the jacket hooks so I reach up and take a handful of the dusty brown pebbles and spill them on the floor because I learned the hard way that he will bite my hand if I hold the kibble too long. While he sniffs around for every last piece of kibble, I hang up my windbreaker and take off my boots in the mud room and put the bag of carrots I didn't eat at the hospital in the refrigerator.

While washing out my lunchbox I think about how Margarita said she was proud of me today. She told me one of her patients thinks I'm very nice and good at what I do. She also told me that I'm a Number 73. She said that being a Number 73 is a good thing and that it means I do a good job and they are so happy to have me here. She handed me an envelope to take home to Mom and Dad so I take it out of my backpack and put it on the front hall table with the rest of the mail that I remove from our mailbox on the front porch.

The ping-pong table is still there and it reminds me of summer with the twins and Robbie and how it is just around the corner even if it means more quiet in the house because Robbie is working on an important project in college and the twins are in Europe taking a train all over the place. It's okay though because I'm busy with work and maybe I will get better than a Number 73 next time I meet with Margarita at the lunch table just the two of us in the middle of the morning when it isn't lunch yet.

I take a snack pack of Chex Mix from the cabinet and walk upstairs with my backpack, which I place on my bed. It is empty now and I will be sure to fill it up before I go to sleep at ten o'clock tonight after dinner and *Full House*. If the twins were here, they would be watching *The Simpsons* and inviting me to join them. I should like *The Simpsons* because they are a cartoon but it is a very fast cartoon with a lot of finger pointing and making fun of and even though the family comes together at the end of every episode it does not feel the same as the family coming together at the end of *Full House* or *Little House* or even *The Brady Bunch*.

I use the bathroom and look around the sink where there is Mom's hairbrush with some of her hair in it. The cap was left off the toothpaste so I have to put it back on. There is a still wet washcloth clumped in the corner of the bathtub and I shake it out and place it on the towel hanger like it should be. Mom and Dad must have been in a hurry for work today because they usually don't leave the bathroom in such a mess like this. By now Cody has stopped following me around, probably because he knows there is no more kibble to eat, so I'm alone in my bedroom upstairs keeping busy with the things I need to do.

Whenever I come home after a day at work I find things

184

that need to be organized and put in the right place. It sometimes feels like when I'm away some of my things move around on their own and give me something to do when I come home. Or maybe Cody is moving these things as a game. But if he had anything to do with it he would be upstairs with me watching and laughing to himself that I'm cleaning up his mess. When I really think about it, there is nobody moving my things around. It is just that I come home and I see things more clearly than when I left in a hurry that morning. So in the quiet house with Cody downstairs and Mom and Dad at the store I get to work organizing my things in their proper place and making sure there is order to everything like my desk clock and my alarm clock that always need a tune-up because it only takes one or two days for them to start telling different times.

As I'm lining up my shoes in order of sneakers to church shoes, I remember that it is June first and that means I need to redo the calendars. It isn't enough for me to do my own calendars like the one on my dresser that has the months and numbers that spin until they say the right date. It is also the calendars all over the house that need catching up because Mom and Dad have been so busy at the store I'm sure they have not noticed. They know it is June first because they have to know this for paperwork at the store but I don't think they have thought about the calendars all over the house like I do.

As I get to each of the calendars I count them in my head. I'm a Number 73 at the hospital and there are seven calendars in our house. That makes it easy to remember because seven is the first number in 73. Even though the twins are far away I still feel like I might get caught sneaking into Kenny's bedroom to change over his calendar. Danny doesn't have a calendar in his bedroom, but I walk in it anyway because he has very interesting pictures on the walls like women in sand on the beach and him playing lacrosse and Robbie's old U2 poster that he took for himself as soon as Robbie went away to college. Walking upstairs to Robbie's room always makes me feel a little sad inside because I miss him and he is away the most of everyone. It has been a long time since Robbie lived upstairs and his calendar is actually from last year but I turn it from May to June anyways. I don't know why in my head but it feels right in my tummy.

After turning all the calendars to June, I reward myself by turning on the television and watching a rerun of *Full House*. It is the one where Becky doesn't get the job and everyone tries to help her out but the biggest help they do is to be there for her when times are tough. They learn that they can't get the job for Becky and that sometimes things don't work out like they should. I like this episode. The pink sweater that Michelle wears is so cute! And DJ is getting so much older she must almost be ready for high school. And the guys are so goofy and they try so hard but they're also just guys so they need to be cut some slack.

But Becky. Becky is just so kind and so lovely and so much like someone I would love to meet in real life even though she does not exist as Becky in real life. Still, she makes me feel good and like there are people on television that real people can also be like. Becky is like Vicki. Their names even sound the same. I feel a pang in my heart when I think about this. It has been a long time since I have seen her and I hope she's all right. I wonder if Paula is still with her. I hope I can see Vicki soon because she's so nice and I like spending time with her like around Lake Waban and in Doris the car and in her garage making stained glass together. Oh, look. A commercial for the *Teenage Mutant Ninja Turtles* movie. I don't think I'll see that one but they look like they are having fun.

The first clue that something is different is when Mike tries to pull into our driveway and there is nowhere to pull into because it is full of cars that all look like they need a wash. "Looks like a party at 63 Brook Street!" I brush him off because it is more important for me to remember what this is all about. I open the back door and the house smells different. Musty and smoky and cologne but not Old Spice. I hear deep voices all around me, but the kitchen is empty. Empty of people, that is. Otherwise it is an absolute mess. I can't even see the breakfast table because of all the chips, boxes of cookies and plastic soda bottles. Robbie is home! And he brought his entire singing group with him. That's right. His singing group is making a CD and they are making it in Boston. Now I know what his important project is all about. Robbie is home with his singing group from college to make a CD. Robbie is home and that makes me feel all right about the mess in the kitchen and the smells throughout the house and the noises that get very loud with handclapping and laughter and also quiet and mysterious like there are some secrets being shared.

I hear feet bounding down the stairs and prepare myself to hug Robbie so I let my backpack slide off my back and wait for him to burst into the kitchen in three...two...one... "*Claire!*" There he is with his broad grin and sparkling eyes and wide-open arms that squeeze around me in a big, all-enveloping hug. *Hi, Robbie! Your singing group is here?* He says that yes his group is here and that if they cause any trouble whatsoever to please let him know. The good thing is that they will be out of the house at six o'clock every night and returning in the early morning to sleep. Apparently, they can only record at night when it is quiet outside so there is no car noise on the recordings. That's probably how they could afford the studio because they couldn't pay for a studio with thick enough walls. I wonder how Robbie is going to manage without getting regular hours of sleep. I know how much that would mix me up to be out of my routine.

As he introduces me to the dozen or so members of his group, I'm struck by how different they are from each other. They have different-sounding voices. Some have beards that they mean to have, some have beards they don't mean to have, some don't have beards at all. One has that beard that's not a full beard that is called a goat or something like that. I don't like that look very much but the person with the goat on his face looks handsome anyway. They all have a young glow to them, even if they are old enough to grow beards and be in college and smoke and drink beer. (I think they thought I wouldn't notice the crushed cans in the corner of the living room and in the wastebasket beneath the kitchen sink.)

They are young in their eyes and skin and they are all degrees of grown-up. It makes it easier to know they are nice and they seem to like me and they promise to stay out of my hair and anytime I want to hear a song, just ask. At that moment, they begin singing a song and they circle around me and get closer and by the end of this love song the most handsome singer with the round glasses and crooked smile with great teeth gets on his knee and holds my hand. He kisses it once the song is over and I feel like Marcia Brady by thinking about not washing it ever again. Yes, it will be a crazy week and I will be frustrated by the disorganization and the mess but I will be a grown-up and I will do my regular thing and not let anything get to me because if this is something that brings Robbie home from college, I will only say yes to everything.

The week is a jungle camp of experiences. As much as Robbie and his group promise to not be in our hair, they create changes to our routines that can't be overlooked. There are the late-night returns home from the Boston studio with the car doors slamming, the arguments on the front porch, the smoking on the terrace and the television showing VCR movies. They sleep everywhere possible, even in Kenny and Danny's bathtub. The bathroom doors are always closed and we are constantly out of milk. The basement becomes a no-go zone because that's where many of them sleep and it's where all of them toss their dirty clothes that would never get washed if Mom didn't start doing it herself after the first few days.

To their credit, they did not have strangers over. They really did leave the house by six o'clock every evening so Mom, Dad and I could enjoy our peace and quiet. They brought us cookies and leftover pizza and they even bought wine for Mom and Dad after the first night at our house. They were always polite and they said please and thank you and they smiled at us and they did random things like one time they handwashed Mom's station wagon. Why they didn't wash their cars instead, I will never know. Their cars remained dirty in our driveway, yet I became used to getting dropped off in the street and looking at those filthy cars with their bumper stickers and Connecticut College window labels because in my heart of hearts I was proud of them.

The Harmonics gave Mom, Dad and me the constant sound of music that never let up because there was always more improvement to be made on the songs they were recording. There was singing and humming and table-drumming and whistling and improvising. There was brainstorming and creating and imagining and envisioning. There was smiling and laughing and struggling and plugging. There was beer drinking, cigarette smoking, swearing and bush peeing. There was eating and spilling and dog feeding and wrestling. There was arguing and debating and fighting and apologizing. There was recording and music making and line noting and graphic designing.

The result of all of this was a CD that would never leave my mom's car radio the entire time Robbie was in college and for years afterwards. One night she was in her car for a long time with the engine running and the headlights off and I finally got impatient and I walked out to the driver's side in the cold and I knocked on the window and she must have been sleeping because she bolted up and rolled down the window and explained to me that things were fine and that she was just thinking about the day she had at work. This must have been a bad day for her, because there were tears on her cheeks and the music was Robbie's solo for 'Don't Let the Sun Go Down on Me' and it was beautiful and sad and had a way of cutting into all of our hearts because it was just so pure and true. At that moment I knew Mom was not sad from work, she was sad from Robbie and she missed him and she missed him not only because he was away in the real world but also because he was away in the world of his adulthood.

No One is to Blame

George has a sister who lives in Framingham, which isn't very far away from where I live with my parents. When George's mother died a few months ago, his father decided to move from South Carolina to be closer to his sister. This means that I see George on a regular basis now. He lives with his father and they have a house that is close to his sister. George's sister is a teacher and she teaches little kids. I think she sometimes forgets to turn off her kid-teaching voice when she talks and it is funny when she uses simple words and a sing-songy voice when she talks to grown-ups like me and George's father.

George and his father are very close. This is because they get along like brothers on a good day and they never argue. George tells me it has always been this way. I think it has gotten better since his mother died. She was sick for a long time and it was very hard for both of them to see her feeling so sick and weak. They spent a lot of time helping her as best they could. He tells me the hardest part was knowing that there was nothing they could do to make her feel healthy again and they could only help her feel like we normally do instead of feeling achy and tired so much of the time. I met George's mom once when we were driving back from my second Disney Cruise and we stopped by his house in

South Carolina. She asked me questions from her bed like how being on such a big boat was different from the boat I sail in on the Cape. She asked about what it was like to always have dogs as pets. She wanted to know about twin brothers and what makes them the same and different.

I always thought George looked a lot like his father. They are both tall with big hands. They have brown hair and the same deep laugh. But when I met his mother, I saw the same eyes. When George's mother squinted, her eyes looked just like George's. It was like I could see George lying in front of me, not his mother. And it was very warming to my heart to be looked at by his mother with the same kindness as when George looks at me. When she squeezed my hands and told me to take care of her baby, I thought that of course I would take care of George because he takes care of me and that way we both take care of each other. George takes care of me when I'm anxious about getting somewhere on time by saying they're not going to hold up the event for me so don't worry about making people wait. He takes care of me when I forget to bring my lunch to Parkland Rec by saying that I will not starve. He takes care of me when I need to be quiet and by myself by letting me be quiet and by myself while he thumbs through the magazines on the coffee table for almost an hour. George tells me I'm taking care of him by being with him during this difficult time and that just being with me is all he wants. Jed used to tell me he wanted things from me like all of my time on the phone, like my hand in his hand, like me to wear clothes that he liked, like for me to let go of my friends because they are a bad influence on me. I don't mean to paint Jed in a bad light. It is just that the more I'm with George the more I think about Jed because with Jed

I didn't have anyone to compare him to and I think it would have helped me and even might have saved that phone from being flushed down the toilet.

"Like your relationship."

Doreen and I are talking upstairs in my bedroom. She just came in on her own, without Robbie, and it is the first time she has ever done this in all of the years I have known her as Robbie's girlfriend. Doreen comes over when Robbie is away like when he lived in New Zealand for a semester. But she does not visit me in my room. She is great to spend time with me, especially when Robbie isn't around. She drives me places and picks me up from Parkland Rec sometimes when Mom and Dad are stuck at the store. She and I talk about basic things that never go further than talking about our day, the weather, how the Red Sox are doing, and what are our plans for the weekend. But she's always nice and she cares about me because she loves Robbie.

Yes, like my relationship. She is good about making comparisons like that and understanding how the phone flushed down the toilet might make me feel. Doreen then tells me to be thankful I have such an amazing boyfriend in George. I want to say he's not my boyfriend because saying you have a boyfriend is a very big deal and I can't believe sometimes I'm in this big deal. But she reminds me that yes, I'm in this big deal because he moved all the way up here to be close to me. *He moved here to be close to his sister.* She gives me a raised-eyebrow look and if she were Vicki she would say "Ummm…someone needs to clean her glasses." I get quiet thinking about how moving up here was not necessary for George and his father to do because they were living together just fine down in South Carolina. I stay quiet, feeling about how moving up here was definitely something they would not have done if it weren't for me.

Doreen stays with me for a long time and we talk about boyfriends and relationships and how they are different from friendships. She talks about boyfriends she had in high school and college and how she learned a lot about herself with each boyfriend she had a relationship with. She then told me about how her friendship with Robbie was the best thing for her over these past few years because it made her realize how deep her love for another person could be. Apparently, Doreen spends a lot of time thinking about my oldest brother. She also tells me very sternly that there is no one else she would rather go camping with, or on a road trip with, or just sit around and drink coffee with. She tells me to never undervalue my brother Robbie because he has the biggest heart of anyone she has ever known and someday he will make someone very happy.

And with that, she left my room and our house and I never saw Doreen again.

But I did see Vicki. And it confused me because she came over without telling me. I don't think she told anyone except Robbie. I'm upstairs in my bedroom organizing my things for our Columbus Day long weekend trip to Maine with my friends and Suzie. As I'm laying out my socks, I hear guitar music play outside. I know it is from outside because it is sounding through my open window that is right above the porch. The sound is clear and beautiful and as I listen closer it becomes two guitars, with one leading the way and the other following. The one following isn't so bad and, in fact, it couples nicely with the clear and beautiful guitar leading the way.

194

I shuffle downstairs two feet at a time, holding the banister like I always do. Before heading outside, I look through the window and I see Robbie with Vicki on the sofa together in the screened-in area of our front porch. By now they have stopped playing and their backs are facing me but I can tell that they are having a very serious discussion and I can imagine the look on Robbie's face is wide-eyed and open-mouthed and the look on Vicki's face is half-eyed and closed mouth. Robbie is the leader in their conversation. Vicki is the follower who nods her head and I'm sure is saying, "Ummm-hmmmm," like she always does, but I can't hear through the window. I know they still don't know that I'm watching them, so I decide to head into the den to watch another rerun of *Full House*.

As I'm just about to turn on the television, I hear the guitars play once again. This time I also hear voices together in harmony with each other and I put down the remote control and just listen. I don't understand the words because to me the words are not the most important part anyway. But I hear the duet and how well Robbie and Vicki are joined together in their music. Vicki used to tell me that music was a way for the soul to express itself. When it is two souls expressing themselves in such close harmony, I believe something special is created. Something strong and supportive like friendship or even love.

Robbie is flopped out like he used to do growing up. He knocked all the stuffed animals and dolls off the sofa and is lying there on his back facing the ceiling and tossing my stuffed Easter rabbit up toward the ceiling again and again and again as he talks. He is talking to me, but he is also I think talking to himself because he doesn't wait for me to respond and he doesn't ask me any questions. He just talks and talks and talks. "I'm writing Mom and Dad a love letter."

Why? Why would Robbie be doing that? I don't need to even try to answer my own question because if I just keep listening to him babble on he will tell me why and more. So through listening to him talk to the ceiling, I pick up pieces like, "They need to know the truth," and "It will be better if they knew," and words like "authentic" and "self-actualized" and lots of the words "love" and "happiness" and "honesty". Deep inside I sense exactly what he is talking about, yet I don't have a word for it. I believe Mom and Dad might not like getting this letter, and I try to forget what Robbie was saying as soon as he leaves my bedroom because if I don't I will not sleep very well at night at all.

I don't need to worry about not sleeping for many nights because Robbie being Robbie decides to write and give the letter to Mom and Dad while at the dinner table. He introduces the ticking time bomb with, "There's something I would like for you to read." He hands it to Mom, who reads with her eyes moving back and forth very quickly and after fifteen seconds says, "I know what this letter says." She and Robbie get into an argument about showing respect for the time he put into it and Dad finally reaches over and takes the letter from Mom and reads it doubly slow as he usually would. As his eyes move back and forth, they become heavier with every line so that once he finishes reading the letter and folding it carefully and sliding it back into its envelope he looks like he has aged at least ten years. When he silently gets up from the table and mutters how he needs to "think about it", he walks like Grandpops and from that point I realize that words have the power to damage people in their bodies and not just their minds. And the months afterwards convince me that they

196

certainly have the power to break and mend hearts.

This should not be news to me. I have seen how words make other people feel happy or sad. When Kate was dealing with those teenagers at CVS, when I had my cousin tell me she outgrew me, when Jed said some of those things he said…all of those words caused feelings of tiredness, sadness and fear to take over. They are not good. But then there is the "You go, girl!" from the sidelines at the Special Olympics. There is the "You're a Number 73," from Margarita. There is the "It doesn't matter what we do as long as we are together" from George.

During those months, I barely saw Robbie. He was working at a local school nearby and he was trying to study for a big test at night. Something about law school and how this test will be the most important one he has ever taken so would we all please show some respect by being quiet? The sense in the house is tight and as the days are getting shorter it is like a blanket of darkness is coming over all of us. In October, Dad starts lighting the wood stove like he often does. In November, Mom starts to write cards and make special food like stuffed turkey and mashed potatoes and beans. All during this time, Mom and Dad spend many hours at the store and they are more quiet than usual because they are processing Robbie's letter in the back of their minds.

I see the letter on their foreheads, though. I feel the frustration at not being able to process it quickly and smoothly. I see the heavy lids and the bleary eyes that try to greet me at breakfast. I'm upset at Robbie for writing the letter and making Mom and Dad get old. But I'm also upset at Mom and Dad for not just taking him at face value and accepting what he had to say because he is an adult and he has the biggest heart of anyone I have ever known and someday he will make someone very happy.

Winter is dark and long and quiet and when I see the twins it is usually for one of their college hockey games or when they are home for a little bit of time during their vacations. Kenny's college is in Vermont and Danny's is in Connecticut. This is meaningful because they are both happy to be at separate colleges when before they were not happy to be at separate high schools. They tried once, in ninth grade, and it did not work well. They would make sure they called each other on the school payphones once a day and it did not take long before the principals decided it was best for them to still be together. This makes sense to me. If I had an identical twin, I would want to be with her even if it meant being confused as the same person sometimes. I would just try harder to express myself for who I am. I would take a lesson from Robbie's playbook, as Dad now likes to say. I can see how Dad is proud of Robbie for "grabbing the bull by the horns". He has been on board with him since reading the letter and now he and Mom are together in their support for Robbie and there will be no more silence and no more hushed conversations at the bottom of the stairs.

Robbie comes back from six months in Mexico and he is joined by his friend Ricardo. They are inseparable. They are lighter together than they are apart and there is a glow they give off when they are doing something like a team. Ricardo wants to get to know me on a deep level. He asks me questions like Margarita at work does. He wants to know things about me that Robbie might not be able to share with him. Things like my dreams, my goals, and how I feel about my work-life balance. That last question is a funny one to me because my work-life balance has been the same every day since I graduated from

St Coletta's. I tell Ricardo about my van driver, Mike, who picks me up at 8:40 and drops me back home at four. I tell him about the clocks and I show him that the kitchen clock and the stove clock are off by a minute and before I even ask, he fixes it. Ricardo seems to understand me like he has known me for a long time. I like how I feel when I'm around him.

After arriving home from work one day, I see Robbie and Ricardo on the porch. Both have guitars in their hands and as I walk up the porch steps and around the ping-pong table I hear music that doesn't sound like the music Robbie usually plays. It isn't happy music but it is strong and real. Ricardo sings in a different language from Mexico, and his eyes are closed and he appears to be lost in the vision of what Mexico is for him. He moves his head back and forth, looking up to the porch ceiling with eyes closed and feet tapping. Robbie follows, his foot also tapping, and I sit in the chair next to them with my eyes wide open and looking at them both with a feeling of joy inside because there is harmony in the two of them that is the most special thing I have seen in a very long time.

Enjoy the Silence

These days my life is pretty quiet. I wake up in my house with Dad already at work and Mom downstairs with breakfast and the *Today* show. We watch together while eating breakfast and she makes sure I have the right lunch for the day ahead. In this way, it feels just as it has felt for the past few years since Kenny and Danny headed off to college. With Robbie in Boston, it isn't that he is too far away. But he isn't here now with the twins and me wolfing down our cereal and looking at our imaginary watches and saying how late we are going to be because look it's already eight o'clock.

I get into my van and the party it always used to be has changed into a library. Everyone is on their iPhones listening to their music or watching their television shows on demand. I don't have an iPhone or iPod or anything like that so it is up to me to talk with Mike, who has even started wearing his own headphones so he can be hands-free. If it is for our safety, then it makes sense but it seems to come with a price because I have no one to talk to. So I look down at my Velcro sneakers or I take out some information sheets from a few weeks ago that were stuffed at the bottom of my backpack. Sometimes Mike takes out his headphones and he asks me what I will be doing today. *The same stuff.* And then we talk about what the same stuff is and how much I like folding things, especially bedsheets, which isn't really true but it keeps the conversation going.

The headphones are called earbuds, and Kate is very clear with me about this. They go in your ear and they play music very clearly. It is as if the music is coming from inside your head, she says, and it is really cool. She has offered her earbuds to me so many times but I can't enjoy them in my ear. They feel funny and then they begin to hurt a bit. Even if they didn't hurt, they would irritate me because they are objects sticking inside my ear. They could tickle and I would still be irritated. It is like an itch I can't scratch unless I don't bother to get the itch in the first place.

This is an interesting quiet because every so often there is laughter coming from Keith or Dwight or there is all of a sudden singing coming from Cathy, who still loves Madonna. Cathy sometimes sings 'Hung Up", which I love because it has some Abba in it, and I imagine the song in my head as she sings the chorus part aloud and off-key. Still, it is amusing and fun to see how overtaken Cathy can be by Madonna. Dwight plays John Madden Football on his phone, which means he jerks his head and grunts throughout the entire van ride. Christine listens to classical music "because it is the only real music out there" and Jeannie listens to The Beatles and The Beach Boys because even though it's old music it makes her happy. Donna doesn't listen to her iPhone much, but she has become tired over the past few years and the van makes her fall asleep and I don't want to be rude and wake her up just because I'm bored. I'm bigger than that.

I see it everywhere, even in church when people are settling into their pews and the first hymn starts playing and we all stand up just before singing and there are still some people looking down to the side and thinking that they are being polite and secret. They are putting their phone on a more important level than Mr. Gallagher. I know that church isn't for everyone and many people go just to get a good attendance record or to give money or to listen to their kids belting out 'All Creatures of Our God and King' with the children's choir. Some give their phones to their kids who are sitting with them and need to be controlled. I don't remember my brothers or me needing a small television set passed over to us in order to get us to pretend to pay attention.

Kate says she gets bumped into a lot more often than she used to at CVS. Actually, she never got bumped into during her first years there. Now everyone is looking for a better deal online so they are wandering around aimlessly. She even misses the packs of teenagers who used to disrupt Aisle 5 because now they are still a pack but they are glued to their phones. A silent mob. Dwight talks about going to Patriots games at Foxboro Stadium and how so many people in the crowd would be looking down on their phones instead of watching the game in front of them. If Granny were still going to Red Sox games, she would be looking down to score the game like always but she would be surrounded by so many other people who are looking at their phones.

I remember being at the local Starbucks and there was a nanny with a little kid and the nanny was watching a movie on her phone and the little kid was trying to get her attention. Whenever he made a noise he was told to shush by the nanny who did not even look up from her phone. Finally, he looked at the wall and he leaned his cheek on it and he started moving it up and down on the wall and then he started licking the wall with his tongue out and his eyes staring at the nanny. He was staring at his nanny and his tongue was lapping up all of the dirt and sneeze and breath and paint on the yellow wall and nobody even noticed…because they were on their phones.

It is especially hard for me to see people texting instead of calling when I know that I can't text because my fingers are too shaky and I can't spell or read very well. I suppose I could have an iPad because they have bigger keyboards. But the screens are so bright and the colors are sharp and they hurt my eyes like I'm sitting too close to the television or like the colors coming out of the iPad are sharp like knives and they give my eyes paper cuts. It is the same with computers. I have never had an easy time with using a keyboard and the screens are so bright. Now everyone watches television on their computers instead of together like when we watched *The Cosby Show* and *Little House* and *The Brady Bunch* and the news about gorillas in Central America. People watch their computers with earbuds in so no one knows what they are watching so no one can have the same feelings as each other. It is just quiet. Very quiet. And very different. Not impossible but definitely different.

And then there is Faith and Light. Christine's mother started this group for us and we meet every Sunday afternoon at her house in Sudbury. I love Faith and Light. It is a chance for my friends and me to sit around and listen to a Bible story and talk about it. Sometimes we learn a lesson from it. Sometimes we just sit there and listen to someone make a connection about it like how it makes them think about their life. Christine's mother will sometimes teach us something from the story. She will also try to get us to think before we speak so we are not just talking to hear the sound of our own voices. This is where Cathy has the most trouble, but we are there to help her learn how to be part of a group. At the end, we always light a candle and we say prayers to people who need to be thought about. They could be people who are sick or sad or anyone who could use a hand because life can be really hard sometimes and we all need to know that we are not alone. Faith and Light proves that we are never alone because we sit in a circle and there is a candle so we can't hide from each other.

Dwight says he wouldn't go if there wasn't food served as well. Fortunately, there is a lot of food served at Faith and Light and we usually roll out of Christine's mother's house with round tummies and feeling ready for a nap. Faith and Light is about God and Jesus and the Bible. It is also about us. It is about our friendships and how we are all here to support each other and to be good to each other and to other people. Some people cry at Faith and Light because they are praying for a family member or a friend. Others just sit and laugh because it is the only time during the week when they feel like they can tell stories that need to be told because they are just plain funny. Most of the time we laugh also, even if we don't know what the point of the story is because watching people laugh usually is contagious.

George goes to Faith and Light, too. He has needed it since his mother died and I think it has been very helpful for him to have a group to share feelings with. George tells great stories about his mom. I enjoy watching his face turn red and shiny when he remembers her taking him to the farmers' market on Saturdays and how she would barter with the people for a better price. Or how she would have peppermint tea at three o'clock every day. This makes me think of Granny and her silver tea with one sugar cube and milk. Sometimes people seem to have a lot more in common than we think they do on the surface. They are like Lake Waban in the wintertime when it looks like it is just a bunch of ice but under the ice are the sleeping fish and the plants and the crayfish and the turtles. There is a lot going on under the surface of Lake Waban in the wintertime, even if Dad and my brothers only thought about the ice for skating.

Even though I have been going to Faith and Light for a long time, I still don't really know what faith is. It is something like hope but there is more to it I think. There is something church-like in faith, something that involves waiting patiently and being silent and knowing that we can't change the world by ourselves. It takes a village and it takes something like magic as well. Light is easy for me to understand because we all have it. It isn't just from the candle, it is from inside all of us and it is up to us to "let it shine, let it shine, let it shine". It is the brightness of the light from the people at church on Christmas Eve that makes me cry during 'O Come All Ye Faithful'. It is a blindness that happens and is so strong and blinding with only the most beautiful feelings that it causes me to cry. This is the opposite of the feeling of brightness from a computer screen, which could make me cry because of painful feelings like paper cuts in my eyeballs. Crying in church at Christmas Eve is my way of feeling the beautiful power of human souls that all have faith inside them and light that shines so bright it can make even the most spiral-eyed and dark-hearted person look up and feel just a little bit better for the first time in ages.

Beautiful Day

No. I can't go today. I feel sick.

Truthfully, I'm terrified.

We have been gearing up for a long time now for my big move to Cross Street, which is a new house on Cross Street at the other end of town. Mr. Gallagher is in charge of Cross Street even happening. He allowed the cellphone company to build a tower inside our steeple and it paid the church enough money to build Cross Street. The house already existed. The church bought it and made it handicap-accessible.

Kate, Keith, Dwight, Cathy and Jeannie will live there with me. I will share a room with Kate. We will also share a bathroom. We will all share a kitchen and make sure no one takes all the food. We will have house parties and watch television together. We will have kids trick or treat on Halloween and we will have a Christmas tree and a menorah for Kate and decorations for birthdays and other celebrations during the year. We will have a garden and grow tomatoes and keep the squirrels out of the birdfeeder. We will learn how to get along every day and every night and we will use what we have been learning at Faith and Light in order to have calm and collected conversations about things that are bothering us. No pets, but maybe someday we will have a cat. That all depends on the rules that our supervisors make. The best thing about this move to Cross Street is that Mike will continue being our van driver. He is driving slowly these days. But he is also driving safely like always.

Today is moving day and I'm scared to my bones.

Everything is packed and ready to go. We put the dolls in boxes to go in the upstairs part of the garage, so they are gone forever. Mom had me pick out my favorite stuffed animals, so I took Gund and Bunny and a few others. I packed my own clothes and made sure to leave some clothes and underwear and things for when I come home to my parents' house to visit. The timing for visits is great because I stopped going to Granny and Grandy's house on Wednesdays a long time ago and it will be nice to spend nights at my old house from time to time.

But I can't leave my old house.

My bedroom walls are mostly bare now. I picked the paint color for my new bedroom and Kate picked it for our new bathroom. I chose yellow for the bedroom and Kate chose blue for the bathroom. They are both soft colors of paint because anything too bright would just keep us awake all the time and probably not be good for the relaxed mood Kate and I are trying to create. It is fun being able to pick paint colors. There are so many! We finally just had to bite the bullet and pick one because as Dad said, we don't have all day. My new bedroom will have hardwood floors! This is something that I know is fancy and important because everyone in television commercials talks about their shiny and new hardwood floors and their friend nods with open mouth and wide eyes, very impressed.

I can't wait to see Juliet's expression when she sees the hardwood floors in my bedroom. It will be fun having her come to visit when the time is right. She is in her own group home in England but that doesn't make me feel any better going away from my real home to a group home of my own. I know I'm being a baby. I know Juliet did this years ago and she still smiles. But I can't just pretend. I can't just say *I'm fine*.

Please just go away, Mom and Dad. Please.

I'm going to miss the bluebirds and the cardinals that use the birdfeeder outside the kitchen window. I'm going to miss the terrace that looks over the hill in our backyard, and the green-and-white striped awning we set up for Kenny and Danny's high school graduation ten years ago. I'm going to miss the vegetable garden and the hedges and the Japanese maple tree. I'm going to miss the sound of classical music through every room on the bottom floor and I'm even going to miss the sound of the *Today* show blaring in the kitchen every morning. Most of all, I'm going to miss seeing my family every day. Not in real life, of course. Kenny is in Paris and Danny is in Hartford and Robbie is in Boston but in pictures when I walk down the front hall stairs, into the den, into the family room, and into the piano room. I will miss seeing my family every day as much as I want to. And I will definitely miss Cody and how he chases after everything and runs away from squirrels like a fraidy-cat.

No, I don't need a doctor. I just need to sleep.

At that moment, I notice a new person in my bedroom and recognize her smell immediately. A mix of cigarettes and mints and perfume. Vicki sits at the end of my bed and just sits. She doesn't say anything for a long time after Mom and Dad have left my bedroom. She just sits there, looking around at my bare walls, my boxes, the few clothes still hanging in my closet for when I visit. She doesn't say anything and she just sits there.

I pretend I don't notice her, but of course she knows that I do and the more I think about how she knows I know she's there the more nervous I get. My tummy begins to ache and for the first time I wish for it to get worse. That is how much I don't want to go to Cross Street.

Time passes by slowly. By the time I feel like the sun must be setting, Vicki starts singing the song about when you've got a friend. The singer whose voice is all from his nose which sounds ugly but it's actually not. In fact, it's a voice that can melt butter. That's what Vicki says and I agree.

Oh goodness, no. Not now. I can't bear to hear this song. I can't hear it from Vicki especially because it is too much. It is my friendship with her. It is my childhood that took place in this house. It is understanding that I'm feeling lonely and could use a friend to come running and see me again. It is telling me that I've got a friend and I know I've got many friends. So many friends. But Vicki, she's my friend since I was little. She is my teacher and my protector. She is my parent who isn't a parent. She is my counselor and my queen of fun times. She keeps singing. Relentlessly and with the unchanged voice that can only belong to her. She keeps singing with that voice and I make the mistake of squinting a look at her and she catches my eye and all of a sudden the floodgates open. I sob for I have no idea how long and Vicki finishes the song. I'm a puddle in my own soon-to-be-old bed and Vicki continues to sing instead of comforting me like her song says!

Once the song stops, however, Vicki leans over and hugs me. She just hugs me and she holds me and she makes me know that she isn't going anywhere until I'm ready for her to go away. It is up to me to get sick of her, she says. It is my call. This whole decision to move to Cross Street was my call, she reminds me. And still it is going to be the hardest thing I've ever done. Harder than the first plane ride to London on my own to see Juliet. Harder than letting Jed go away to grow up. Harder than graduating from St Coletta's and harder than watching my brothers all leave the house in order to build houses of their own.

That is the magic in Vicki's words. Right there. My brothers have already left. My home will never be the same again. I can walk around and reset the clocks and put the cap on the milk and make sure the matching mittens are in their right bins until the cows come home. But my brothers are not coming home. They will never come home and now it is my turn to not come home. Mom and Dad will be fine here with Cody. They will visit, because as Mom says, Cross Street is only four point three miles away. (But who's counting? Dad jokes every time she makes this observation.)

I'm beginning to feel a little better.

"Good."

Yes, it will be.

Dwight is always the last one to the dinner table. It isn't that hard to get downstairs when called, is it? He is holding us all up and he knows it but for some reason he just can't be on time. But when he enters the kitchen, he is wearing his old Patriots jersey with 'Bledsoe' on the back and he grins wide and I just want to give him a hug. I don't get myself sometimes.

The beans were cut, the potatoes mashed, and the ham put in the oven. There is a special treat from Emack & Bolio's in the freezer for dessert. Our supervisor, Sinead, helps as everyone gets their plates and loads them up. I notice Dwight putting extra mashed potatoes on his and he catches my eye and he pushes a spoonful off his plate back into the bin. There we go. There is hope for him still.

We sit around the table and eat like a pack of wolves. It reminds me of my brothers and the way they would eat even though it's not a race, as Dad says. Every meal, that is, except for the liver and onions dinner that now makes me smile every time I think about Sandy throwing up.

We have meals and bedtime down to a system. Keith loves to do dishes, so that is his main job. Dwight vacuums and folds laundry. Cathy makes sure the grocery list is updated. Kate is in charge of the mail and making sure everything is on the right hooks in the front hall. Jeannie makes sure everyone keeps their feet off the coffee table when watching television and she also makes sure the bathrooms are clean. I'm in charge of preparing the dinner, which tonight meant cutting the beans and mashing the potatoes, which are things I've done since my summers with Gammy and Grandpops. I also make sure the clocks are on time here in this house and it feels very good to know that everyone appreciates my quirks about time and routine and neatness. If there is anything living together has taught me it is that everyone has their quirks. Jeannie laughs at everything. Cathy is always right (even when she's wrong) and she needs everyone's shoes to be lined up from darkest to lightest. Kate doesn't know when to stop when she teases people. Dwight doesn't know how to be on time for anything, especially dinner. Keith sleeps through his alarm almost every morning. If that is the worst of it, then I'd say our differences are easy to handle.

Don't You (Forget About Me)

Oh, the number of people who are here – for me! I'm at the Lake Waban Club and the room is perfect because a whole wall is glass and it looks out on Lake Waban while the sun is just beginning to set. My fortieth birthday is a big deal for me, but also it seems for my family and my friends. Robbie is here with Ricardo, and they are having a deep conversation with Uncle Jude and Aunt Penny. Kenny is here with his girlfriend, Jenny, and they are talking with Keith and Cathy. Danny is also here with his wife, Amy, and they are watching Dwight show them his new Patriots tattoo, which is on his upper arm. He is very proud of it. Mom and Dad are talking with many people and my friends are clustered together with their Cherry Coke with extra cherry, their water "with gas" (that always makes us giggle), their ginger ale and their Sprite.

The mood in the room is as colorful as my confirmation. In fact, Mr. Gallagher is here, in a wheelchair like Donna uses. Even in the wheelchair he is an overpowering figure of kindness and understanding. The shaking has moved to his head and his wife, Ann, is in charge of moving him around because I don't think he can do it himself. Mom comes over to me in a flash, telling me I need to circulate because after all this is my party and everyone is here to see me. That is fine, I think, I can do this. Everyone here is a friend and everyone here is smiling. This will be easy, even for me.

The party is a blur but I remember everyone mixing around with ice cubes in their drinks. Kenny carries the most impressive camera and flash I have ever seen and I just know that his pictures will turn out great. Robbie was able to get the Harmonics together and they performed three songs and the last song was my favorite because it had a solo by my favorite singer with the round glasses and the crooked smile. Somehow we get the message to sit down at our tables and enjoy the dinner planned for us. There are fifteen tables with eight people at each one. That is a lot of people! And a lot of food to prepare also. I think about this while George takes the seat next to me. He looks so handsome and he has put up with so much stuff about this party. Anyone else would have walked away, but not George. He remains my gentle giant.

Dad and Mom stand up first and they make a toast about me that remembers when I was a little girl and used to paint seashells on the porch overlooking the river and look at how far I've come! I appreciate their saying all those nice words and more, but I'm also glad when they sit down again so we can eat and the spotlight of attention can get off yours truly. But then Robbie, Kenny and Danny get up and they make a very emotional toast about what it was like to have me as an older sister and how it taught them that there is no such thing as a bad day when your sister has a disability. The tears in Robbie's eyes especially give me goose bumps, and there is something deep about seeing my three brothers stand together as adults with their own lives. Still, I'm glad when they all sit down because I really want to get out of the

213

spotlight. But then Carl Hudson stands up with a story about me at their house in Maine and how I reset all the clocks to the right time "according to Claire". The room is laughing like crazy, and I can feel the walls shaking. Inside, I am shaking also because I can't have more attention on me. These toasts need to stop. But instead, I soon find out that they are just beginning.

Vicki tells stories about Doris and leads the entire room in "How happy we are, how *happy* we *are!*" My cousin Rachel talks about how she recognized that I was her friend for life even once my specialness emerged (I have never thought about the word "specialness" but I think I like it). Richard says that I'm his hero. Quiet and reserved Juliet says I'm her best friend. (Did I mention that Juliet took three days off from her home all the way in England to be here tonight?) Cathy says, "No, Claire is *my* best friend! In this country, anyway!" Christine says I'm *her* best friend and her spiritual light. Dwight says I'm the best person to watch the Patriots with because I always make sure the chips bowl is full. Jeannie says I'm crazy and cool and she wants to be just like me when she grows up. Margarita says that I'm more than 73 points. I'm off the charts! Suzie tells everyone that she could lose everyone but she knows that I will always be found. Joyce says, "This is obvious but Claire has a lot more under the surface than it appears." And on and on and on.

Once the night-time has fully blanketed the view of Lake Waban through the floor-to-ceiling wall of glass, I get the feeling that it is time for me to make my toast. The entire time while my food has been getting cold I have been thinking about what to say to everyone. I stand up, look at my watch, and Carl Hudson yells out, "Hey, Claire! Do you have the time?" Before I can answer *it's 7:14*, the entire room is laughing and at that moment I realize that everyone really knows me. I haven't even said anything yet but everyone knows me and everyone is here to celebrate my fortieth birthday with me. Because of this, and because the DJ just started my favorite Madonna song, the one with the choir at the beginning, the one that always makes me happy when I think about growing up, I know that I'm going to be all right.

Lightning Source UK Ltd.
Milton Keynes UK
UKHW041432210821
389240UK00004B/60